Nora's Redemption

by

Carol Henry

The Lobster Cove Series

This is a work of fiction. Names, characters, places, and incidents are either the product of the author's imagination or are used fictitiously, and any resemblance to actual persons living or dead, business establishments, events, or locales, is entirely coincidental.

Nora's Redemption

Cover Art by *Tina Lynn Stout*

The Wild Rose Press, Inc.
PO Box 708
Adams Basin, NY 14410-0708
Visit us at www.thewildrosepress.com

Publishing History
First Champagne Rose Edition, 2019
Print ISBN 978-1-5092-2696-2
Digital ISBN 978-1-5092-2697-9

The Lobster Cove Series
Published in the United States of America

He wished he had more time. But damn, he was desperate. He had an important call coming in and needed phone coverage this morning.

"Look, my current hire won't be in until eleven, if then, and I'm expecting an important call from the Society of Marine Consultants. I need to meet a client and will be out on the ocean this morning."

"Wait a minute. Are you asking me to stay and babysit the phone for a few hours? Or are you offering me the job?"

"How about you sit and mind the office, become familiar with your surroundings, and we'll discuss a full-time position when I get back at noon? We'll go to lunch and work out the details."

"Are you serious?"

"What do you have to lose?"

"Aren't you worried I'll walk off with everything, screw things up, or damage your reputation with a few phone calls?"

"If I was worried, I would have shown you the door the minute you walked in. So are you game? I need to leave. I don't want to, literally, miss the boat."

"Is there a coffee machine with cream and sugar available somewhere in the building?"

"Yes. And fresh donuts from the bakery around the corner. Help yourself."

"Thanks. My name is Nora Spears, by the way. I'm assuming you are Gavin Redmond? The owner and my morning employer?"

"So much for my own communication skills. Sorry, Ms. Spears. I do appreciate your help this morning. If you decide to bail on me, make sure you lock the door on the way out."

Dedication

To my faithful readers who can't get enough
of my Lobster Cove Novels—
I couldn't leave you hanging without finding out
what happened to Nora Spears after her big meltdown
at the cemetery in *Juelle's Legacy*.
Thanks for your love and continued support.

Chapter One

"I am so totally ashamed of my behavior at the cemetery." Nora crossed her legs, leaned back in the yellow Adirondack chair, and closed her eyes. She sighed, shook her head, and made a feeble attempt to hold back the tears so her best friend, Jackie Edmonton, wouldn't see her humiliation.

"Oh, my God, Jackie, I was so stunned over Sebastian's death I totally lost it when I saw his wife standing there next to his mother. I was convinced Juelle actually had the doctors take him off life support and killed him."

The day was bright but cool for mid-May along Pier Two. The umbrella over their café patio table in front of the coffee hut did little to keep the sun shaded as it sparkled off Lobster Cove's coastal bay. Nora flipped her sunglasses back over her bloodshot eyes, reached for her tumbler, and took a sip of the sweet tea. It did little to quench her thirst. She set her glass on the table and met her friend's sympathetic gaze.

Gad, she'd been such fool.

"Oh, my God, Nora, that was a year ago. You were distraught," Jackie reminded her. "You thought the low-life, wife-cheating bozo loved you. He was the man you were going to share the rest of your life with, only to have his life snuffed out at the hands of his wife. Or so you thought at the time."

1

Jackie lifted her frosty glass of iced tea and took a deep swallow. "You know as well as I it was his own damn fault."

She smiled at Jackie's words. They'd been friends since college, and Jackie was always upbeat, making it hard for Nora to be in the doldrums whenever they were together.

"It was my fault he took the boat out in the first place," she said, gazing out over the bay. "If I hadn't pushed him to get the divorce from Juelle like he'd promised, he wouldn't have gotten angry with me and gone to sea so late at night."

"You didn't know he'd be reckless enough to go out with a storm brewing. Besides, you had every right to push him for a divorce. He told you he loved you. Told you he was practically single. He lied to you."

"Still, that's not who I am, Jackie. You know I don't go around breaking down in front of everyone like a desperate despot or call people names. People think I'm the worst Jezebel in the world because I fell in love with a married man, for God's sake."

"Jezebel is an ancient term, girlfriend. Besides, Sebastian has been gone for more than a year. Time to let it go." Jackie waved her hand in the air, then pointed her index finger at her friend. "Time to move on."

"I know. You're right. I've told myself a million times how pathetic I acted in front of the entire town. But I loved him, Jackie. You can't turn the love button on and off to ease the depth of loneliness, angst, and emotional heartache you live with on a daily basis when you lose someone. Facing each day alone is a challenge."

"You're right. I'm sorry. So what are you going to

do?"

"Good question. First I need to find another cottage to rent—preferably not in Lobster Cove."

She would miss the Cove despite a number of people giving her the cold shoulder since her outburst at Sebastian's funeral. Lobster Cove was a warm, cozy town, and she'd settled in over the last few years.

"I need to find a job that pays a lot more than I'm earning at the moment. Preferably one where I can use my business degree and earn enough to start my own accounting business. It's getting harder and harder to come up with the rent for the cottage, not to mention finding an accounting position around here with the income I need. I've decided to look for something around the Bar Harbor area. Maybe I can find a temporary apartment there, as well."

"I'm sorry, Nora. I didn't realize things were so dire that you needed to find someplace else to live."

She'd never told Jackie she had felt like a kept woman, living on the outskirts of Lobster Cove with Sebastian. He'd insisted on paying the rent for the up-market cottage he swore she deserved. It'd taken her too long to surmise it was Sebastian's way of making sure he had access to her whenever he wanted. A secret tryst where his friends and family would be none the wiser to his comings and goings. She'd been so naive. Stupid. And in love.

"What do you plan to do?" Jackie prodded, the ice tinkling in her glass as she lifted it to her lips.

"I don't know. I saw an advertisement with a company that's recently reopened its doors in Bar Harbor. Redmond's Marine Resource Management. It's a marine biology technical advising company. They're looking for a receptionist/accountant. The pay and hours sound impressive. It's certainly much more than I'm making with all the part-time positions I've managed to find. Even though it's not my dream job, I'm thinking of applying so I can at least pay this month's rent and save enough for a down payment on a new place."

"Why don't you stay where you are until you can afford to buy a home?"

"Well, for one thing, the sleazy landlord has offered to barter with me for the rent. I'm not that desperate for a man, and especially not Chuck."

"You've got to be kidding?" Jackie leaned forward, drained her iced tea, and shook her head.

"Nope. After Sebastian's death, Chuck made it very plain he was willing to fill in for him any time I was in need."

"The scumbag."

"That's putting it mildly." She'd had to fend off Chuck's advances many times, especially when he came to collect the rent.

"With your business degree, you should be able to land any job you want. I know for a fact you're so organized. You cross all your Ts and dot all your Is. You know me—I'm the world's worst scatterbrain. Me and computers and numbers don't compute."

"Not true, Jackie. You might not be a techie geek, but you do get the job done. You don't give yourself enough credit."

"You don't have to say that because we're friends."

"You know me better than that. I don't hold back, as you've been witness to at the cemetery. Thankfully, Juelle and her new husband moved to Hawaii, and I don't have to worry about running into them every time I turn around."

"Like I said, the good citizens of Lobster Cove have other juicy tidbits to focus on—I'm sure you've heard all about poor Katelyn and that Sven character?"

"Don't know the whole story about Katelyn, but heard Sven followed his parents and moved lock, stock, and barrel to Norway and hasn't returned. I heard they sold their flower shop, too. It's good to know the burg's focus is elsewhere, and its citizens are no longer flapping about me and Sebastian. Although, I still get those sideways looks every once in a while."

"Told you the Lobster Covians have jumped on the next tasty morsel. So what's your plan?"

"Chuck stopped by again Monday night and gave me an ultimatum. I have until the thirty-first to either pay this month's rent or move out. I need to find a cheaper place to live. I'm going to work on my résumé tonight. Maybe drop it off along with my application at Redmond's and a couple other places tomorrow morning. In any case, whatever I do will depend on me landing a job with enough to cover rent, as well as living expenses. If I don't get a job right away, I'll be living on the street. I'll have to start all over again. Even if it means working two jobs to help me get by."

"You'll get something. You're good at what you do," Jackie reassured her.

"You don't have to say that because we're friends."

"When have I ever said anything to please someone?" Jackie raised her empty glass across the table. "Here's to honesty."

"To honest friendship." She nodded as they clinked their tumblers in agreement. "I can always count on you to brighten my day, Jackie. Thanks for meeting me for lunch today."

"No problem. But if I don't get a move on, I'm going to have two angry boys on my hands. Timmy and Cody hate being late for their soccer games. Their team is in the winner's circle. They made me promise I'd pick them up from my mom's early so they could get to practice before the game. They love visiting her, but when it comes to soccer, those two boys' priorities change on a dime."

"Where's Brad?"

"He left at noon for a job in Portland. He won't be back until tomorrow. We'll Skype the game for him. Say, if you aren't doing anything around five o'clock, why not stop by and check out the game?"

"Like I said, I'll go over my résumé, not to mention get my mindset prepared for tomorrow. I know first impressions mean a lot, even in today's society, and even if it's a receptionist's position. I want to make the best good first impression possible. Some things never change."

"You'll nail it."

"Tell the boys I said hi and good luck. I'll catch the next game. Promise."

****

The following morning, equipped with her résumé, she locked the cottage door, made her way along the sidewalk to her car, and stopped short—her shoulders slumped. A flat tire? Really? Could anything else go wrong this morning? At least her car was still parked in the driveway. But her Auto Club membership had expired six months ago, and she hadn't renewed. Having to pay rent and eat, she'd had to cut back on other expenses. Her membership being one of them.

Not wanting to contact her landlord, who was already giving her alternate choices on how to pay her rent, she called Jay's Automotive in Lobster Cove. Although they were busy, Marge Henkins, the office receptionist, assured her they'd have someone out there early afternoon, one o'clock at the latest. By two, Frank arrived and temporarily fixed the tire. Unfortunately, her plans to apply for jobs were cancelled for the day.

"You'll need to get yourself a new tire real soon." Frank shook his head apologetically. "I wouldn't wait too long if I were you. In fact, if you want, I can tow this here vehicle back to the shop and get ya a new one. From the looks of things, ya might want to have maintenance done while it's there."

"I'm sorry, Frank. I don't have the finances at the moment." She cringed and shrugged her shoulders. "I'll make an appointment with Jay in a couple days. I trust you to have done a great job on the tire today. It should keep me going for a couple more days, won't it?"

"Fingers crossed. I'll see ya in a couple days, then." He took out his billing pad, scribbled on it, handed her the original, and kept the duplicate invoice.

"Thanks for your help. I really do appreciate you coming out today on such short notice."

"No problem, Nora. It's what I do. You have a good day."

Frank walked around his tow truck, jumped into the cab, backed out, and drove down the street. She stood, bill in hand. How the hell was she going to pay this? With any luck, her tire would hold out and get her to Bar Harbor so she could drop off her application at Redmond's tomorrow morning before it was too late to apply.

"Hey, sweet thing, why didn't you give me a call? I would've come out and helped ya with that tire."

Aaagggghhhh! Chuck. Just what she needed.

"Thanks, Chuck, but everything is under control."

"Yeah, but I'd 'a fixed it for nothing."

Sure, but he'd be wanting something she wasn't willing to give in return. Something she wasn't about to give him—now or ever!

Nora knew better than to head back to the house. Chuck would be sure to follow her, hoping she'd give in to his pathetic advances. Another reason she couldn't wait to find another place to live. He'd pestered her since Sebastian's death, hoping she'd transfer her affections to him. Wasn't going to happen. She might have made a mistake with Sebastian, thinking she was in love with him, but she wasn't stupid enough to latch on to Chuck, or any man, for sexual favors.

She slid inside her car and started the engine. She had to escape Chuck's unwanted advances, even if it was for a couple hours. She'd drive to the top of Acadia and contemplate her next move. The view over the expanse of Frenchman Bay and the Atlantic from Cadillac Mountain was always soothing.

She backed out of the drive, hit the gas, and left Chuck standing in the middle of the driveway, waving. A cheesy smile on his face. She ignored him, vowing to find another place to live ASAP, regardless of whether or not she could afford the rent. She was going to stop and buy the latest local paper and see if there were any apartments available. She needed to move out soon, even if she had to stay at a hotel or B&B for a few days.

Nora stopped at Jay's Automotive, picked up the

latest Lobster Cove Anchor News, and then took the long route to Cadillac Mountain. The weather was clear, so the view would be spectacular. It was one of the most restful places in the area where one could contemplate life and relax.

She turned onto Route 3, until she came to the visitor center and the Park Loop Road. She circled around the eastern portion of the island and then turned right onto the one-way byway through the forested area. Once past Bear Brook, she drove on up toward the Overlook and Lookout Point. Deciding to pull into the Overlook's circular drive, she parked, left the engine running, and scanned the panoramic view overlooking Frenchman Bay. The late afternoon sun was still high overhead, the air warm, and the gentle breeze cooling. A cruise ship had sailed into the Bay where it would dock closer to Bar Harbor. White sails dotted the ocean, and below, waves washed up against a craggy, rocky shoreline.

Thoughts of Sebastian, the night they'd argued over the divorce, and the accident niggled her brain. She'd tried to visit him in the hospital, but the family had kept vigil, and she wasn't allowed in to see him. Her heart ached at the thought of his death and the part she'd played. She'd felt she had been as much at fault for his death as his wife. But now she knew better. He'd been a lousy cheat. He'd never intended to get a divorce. It was after his funeral and the spectacle she'd made of herself that she'd discovered he had been seeing someone else, as well.

She put the car in reverse and continued toward Thunder Hole. A touristy spot where the trapped air made a thundering noise when the waves crashed through the rock chamber and forced the air out on the other side. As usual it was packed with tourists enjoying the thunder and spray, while kids climbed down on the boulders to enable the spray to wash over them.

She continued, slowing her vehicle as the road wound around the coast of Otter Point, Little Hunter's Beach, and then wound back into the wooded trail. Birch, aspen, oak, and spruce grew tall and full around Jordan Pond. The traffic pattern changed to accommodate vehicles going in either direction. Taking calming breaths, she enjoyed the seclusion of the forested land before turning the car onto Cadillac Mountain Road. The passage wound upward for a spell before she arrived at the parking lot on the left. She pulled in, turned the ignition off, stepped out, and entered the gift shop where she bought a coffee. She found a spot on the bare rock face sprinkled with clusters of three-toothed cinquefoil flowers and sat.

The bright sunshine sparkled off the ocean down below. Bar Harbor lay sprawled out along the coast. To the left, the small community of Lobster Cove hugged the bay. McClintock and McClintock Lobster Company's building was visible. The large white structure stretched along Pier One. Their fishing trawlers were entering the inlet with their catch of the day. Juelle and her new husband, Hunter McClintock, had inherited the company. The old family business should have been Sebastian's. Not that it made any difference at this point. Besides, Sebastian hadn't cared much for managing operations, and instead, loved being out on the water.

She crossed her ankles, reached for the newspaper,

and opened it to the property listings. She needed to find an affordable apartment or cottage. But the Lobster Cove Anchor's listings were minimal, and nothing appealed. She let out a deep sigh and decided she'd have to call Jessica Martin Real Estate Agency tomorrow and see if she had something available in her price range. Although, what that price range was depended on what job she was able to secure in the next few days.

She took a few minutes to lean back and soak up the peace and tranquility enveloping her as other visitors to the mountain wandered the summit. Taking in one of Maine's top scenic sites, she checked her watch. If she headed back down to Lobster Cove, she'd have plenty of time to make Jackie's boys' game and still have time to go over her résumé one last time before she shopped it around tomorrow. And hope she didn't have any more car troubles.

Or have Chuck waiting for her when she pulled in the driveway.

Chapter Two

Nora pulled into the elementary school parking lot and walked behind the building to the soccer court and the game already in progress. Jackie was easy to spot. Her voice rose above the crowd as she cheered Timmy and Cody on as they ran downfield toward their team's goal. Not having brought her own camp chair, she settled on the ground next to her friend.

"What's the score?" she asked, scanning the field for Timmy and Cody's jersey numbers.

"Don't ask. The other team is ahead by two points, and it's already the second half."

"I thought they were the winning team?"

"Hush. We all have our down time. They'll catch up. We have a half hour left. And look," Jackie said, pointing downfield, "our team has the ball under control."

Nora sat in silence, watching the players kick the ball back and forth, first one side of the field, then the other. The teams alternated controlling the ball. She felt as if she were at a tennis match as she swung her head from side to side. She spotted the players sitting on the bench on the opposite side of the field, and the coaches standing next to them. One in particular stood out. Tall, dark, and handsome. She'd seen him before but had no idea who he was or where she'd seen him. Still, his stature and concentration on the game was striking.

A sudden bout of cheering ensued, bringing her back to focus on the game and Jackie shooting from her seat and screaming.

"Did you see that? Timmy just got the first goal for the team. Yay, Timmy! You go, team!" Jackie sat back in her camp chair, her smile a mile wide. "Whew. We need a few more goals to nail this."

"Sorry, I missed it. I was trying to figure out who the guy is over there next to their coach. He sort of looks familiar."

"Their assistant coach. He looks familiar because you've probably seen him here when you've come to the games." Jackie continued to keep her eye on the players as they kicked the ball downfield. "He isn't here often, but when he is, he tends to stand in the background. Oh, look, Cody has the ball heading for the goal."

Nora turned back to the game and cheered along with Jackie as Cody kicked the ball into the goal, tying the game.

****

Gavin Redmond wondered if he'd ever find a competent receptionist/accountant. Three tries in less than a year wasn't a satisfying track record. And his recent hire was missing in action. Again. Maybe reopening the agency in Bar Harbor hadn't been such a good idea after all.

He slapped the latest round of applications on top of his desk and ran his fingers over his face and through his hair. Dammit! He didn't have time to teach these youngsters how to answer an office phone professionally, add and subtract, or even how to use a spreadsheet. They were all adept at playing games on their electronic gadgets or texting when they should be working. Having to yell over whatever was blaring in their ear buds did nothing for a harmonious office environment. He needed someone who paid attention to detail, had good communication skills, and didn't snap their gum to the latest rap music's syncopated beat, or whatever they were listening to when they were on their phone. He needed someone who took their job seriously. He would be ever so much more ecstatic if that person, man or woman, not only knew something about dealing with people, but was knowledgeable about accounting and Maine's coastal environment.

Was he asking too much?

His coffee had gone cold. He drained the dregs, pushed his black leather office chair away from his desk, and stood. What to do? Not one applicant warranted an interview. Still, he needed to call each one and set up appointments for interviews. Who knew what hidden talent wasn't evident in a résumé? Their references were lukewarm at best, but he needed someone ASAP.

The bell over the office door tingled. Damn, he didn't have time for this. He had a meeting on the other side of the island in forty-five minutes, and he hadn't gotten his act together yet. And thanks to his latest hire having overslept and not planning on coming in until eleven, he was stuck between a rock and a hard place as his grandfather always said. He was more than likely going to have to close shop for the day. He shook his head, rose, and took his time going to the front office to see who had arrived. Hopefully it wasn't another applicant his sister, Bethany, had sent his way.

When he entered the front office, he stopped in his

tracks. Good Lord! A tall, willowy blonde who looked vaguely familiar, or maybe she simply resembled all the other applicants his sister had sent his way lately. The woman's blue eyes, surrounded with black mascara, were so bold they were almost piercing. Her hair, swept up on top of her head, accentuated her blemish-free skin that glowed in the early morning light streaming through the large office windows. She was dressed in a casual-business, pastel-peach dress. It reminded him of a conch shell. The young woman wore a matching jacket trimmed in soft aqua. It had been an obvious attempt to hide her sexy body but instead highlighted it.

He hoped she wasn't here to apply for the job, especially if she was anything like the last three blondes who had walked in off the street yesterday. Once they got past his sister's vetting and sat down for an interview with him, they'd become flirtatious as if that were enough to land them the job. According to his sister, their looks alone were enough to obtain the position. He knew what Bethany was up to. She was attempting to find him a replacement for his deceased wife. Had she sent yet another young blonde bombshell his way?

"May I help you?" He stood in the doorway, hands in pockets, feet slightly apart, trying to place where he had seen her before. He jingled the keys in his pocket, waiting for her to get on with it so he could send her on her way and get back to work.

"I hope so. I'm here to drop off my application for the job you advertised."

Just his luck. He checked his watch and sighed for the zillionth time in the last two hours. "Did Bethany send you?"

"Bethany? I don't know a Bethany. The employment agency assured me you haven't hired for the position yet."

"Have you a working knowledge of Excel?"

"Excuse me?"

"Excel. Microsoft application. Do you have any computer skills?"

"Of course. Otherwise I wouldn't be applying for the position."

"What other credentials do you have?"

"A MS degree in Business Management, which includes accounting."

He raised an eyebrow. She already sounded more qualified than any of the applicants' files he'd finished going through five minutes ago.

"How well do you know the area? Bar Harbor? Lobster Cove? The island? The surrounding coast?"

Where the hell had he met her? He was sure he knew her.

"Depends on what you mean by 'how well.' I've worked temp for three smaller businesses in the area over the past three years. I'm looking for something permanent. My references are listed in my application. I've lived in the area for five years and have hiked the trails along the coast." She retrieved a folder from her shoulder bag and offered it to him.

"Do you know anything about Maine's coastal marine life?" He accepted the folder and placed it on the desk in the small reception area where they stood facing each other. "How are you with social skills, communication? Can you answer a phone without snapping gum, take a message, and organize a meeting with five or more people at the same time?"

"Excuse me? Is this an interview? I hadn't expected to be interviewed on the spot. But just so you know, I don't chew gum—bad for the teeth."

"I'm desperate. I have a meeting"—he looked at his watch again—"in fifteen minutes. What are your plans for the day?"

"Excuse me?"

"Are you free this morning?"

She hesitated, taking him in with a piercing, thoughtful stare before answering. "I can be, if necessary."

Her answer was tentative. Showed she wasn't ready to do anything he asked in order to get the job. Although he'd hoped she would be agreeable to fill in until his temp arrived.

She took a step back. "What do you have in mind?"

At least she was confident enough, or brazen enough, to not turn and run out the door. Bravo for her to stay and face his off-the-wall questions. He wished he had more time. But damn, he was desperate. He had an important call coming in and needed phone coverage this morning.

"Look, my current hire won't be in until eleven, if then, and I'm expecting an important call from the Society of Marine Consultants. I need to meet a client and will be out on the ocean this morning."

"Wait a minute. Are you asking me to stay and babysit the phone for a few hours? Or are you offering me the job?"

"How about you sit and mind the office, become familiar with your surroundings, and we'll discuss a full-time position when I get back at noon? We'll go to lunch and work out the details."

"Are you serious?"

"What do you have to lose?"

"Aren't you worried I'll walk off with everything, screw things up, or damage your reputation with a few phone calls?"

"If I was worried, I would have shown you the door the minute you walked in. So are you game? I need to leave. I don't want to, literally, miss the boat."

"Is there a coffee machine with cream and sugar available somewhere in the building?"

"Yes. And fresh donuts from the bakery around the corner. Help yourself."

"Thanks. My name is Nora Spears, by the way. I'm assuming you are Gavin Redmond? The owner and my morning employer?"

"So much for my own communication skills. Sorry, Ms. Spears. I do appreciate your help this morning. If you decide to bail on me, make sure you lock the door on the way out."

"Do you have a number I can call in case I have a question?"

"It's on my business card in the card holder on the corner of the desk. But use it only if it's an emergency. I don't like to answer the phone while I'm driving. I value my life too much. And I'm not always reachable when I'm out on the water."

Nora Spears walked past him, retrieved a card, studied it, and then flung her shoulder bag over the arm of the chair behind the white-top Steelcase desk.

"Coffee?"

"Through the alcove to the left. Enjoy."

And without another word, he pulled his car keys from his pocket and walked out of the office. He couldn't lose contact with his newest client. Business had become steady, but his reputation for his timeliness and attention to detail was always on the line. He was in the process of rebuilding the company after his father's death, and hopefully would leave it financially viable for his family. Although a family didn't seem likely since Celina's death. His appointment with the CEO of McClintock's, the major fishery in Lobster Cove, was a make-or-break deal to his company. He didn't want to start off being a no-show.

****

Nora stood, mouth agape. What had she gotten herself into? Gavin Redmond. Who'd have thought? Sebastian had mentioned him a number of times, and she'd seen him from afar along the docks but never paid him any attention until last night at the soccer game. She'd admired his confident demeanor and his tall, fit stature. His military exploits had been rumored about town. Seeing the man up close—those piercing ocean-blue eyes, full lips, long nose, and a deep-brown, military-style hair cut that was growing out and hugged his ears—brought a smile to her insides that hadn't been there in a long time.

The man was all business. As interviews went, this was one for the record. Jackie was never going to believe that she was working for *the* Gavin Redmond, one of Bar Harbor's local war heroes. She really needed the caffeine.

The quietness in the snug but comfortable-looking room buzzed eerily in her ears. The noise from her heels as they clicked on the wide wooden floorboards was a shock to her already stunned nerves. She lifted her heels and continued across the floor on her tiptoes as she made her way toward the alcove.

The niche had been converted into a modern compact kitchen complete with all the bells and whistles, including a minibar. The coffee maker's light was on, and an assorted supply of flavored coffee pods were in a wicker basket next to it. And sitting next to it, as promised, was another basket lined with a red-lobster-designed tea towel filled with scrumptious-looking muffins. What a way to start the day.

Choosing a hazelnut coffee pod, she inserted it in the machine, positioned the cup on the coffee platform, and hit the start button. The fresh coffee aroma mingled with a hint of hazelnut was calming. She smiled. *Yes*! Things were improving. She added two sugar packets, an unhealthy helping of half and half, snatched a coffeecake muffin, a paper plate and napkin, and headed to her new workspace in the front office.

Actually, she needed the caffeine to help clear her mind and figure out what she was doing falling under Gavin Redmond's spell so fast, otherwise why had she agreed to fill in for him this morning? She hadn't thought twice before accepting his offer. Okay, so Jackie had told her, via the grapevine, that his wife had died of cancer, and he was widowed. But a man of his stature and sexy good looks? He wasn't bound to be on the eligible bachelor market for long.

She looked around the room as she devoured the muffin and practically inhaled the caffeine. Between the desk, the studio couch, and three easy chairs assembled around an oblong coffee table, it was an inviting, homey atmosphere. It was an older building, the pine wood wainscoting typical New England. The wallpaper, an old paisley-print pattern, on closer inspection, was of sea-nymphs frolicking in tiny spritzes of water. How appropriate for a marine biologist's establishment. The man must have a sense of humor, or he was a romantic.

The huge store-front window provided an awesome view of the street and the bay beyond. She took a moment to enjoy the breathtaking view while she enjoyed the coffee. Then she explored the desk, its contents, the computer, and files, playing snoops-the-lawyer. If Gavin Redmond was going to interview her when he returned, she wanted to know a bit more about the business and whether or not she wanted the job.

The computer module was to the right, the screen facing away from the window and the sun. She scrolled over several files on the screen and was ready to open one when the bell over the front door rang. She jumped, then automatically went into professional mode and stood to address the young girl who entered.

"May I help you?"

"Yes, I'm here to drop off my application for the position Mr. Redmond posted. His sister told me to bring it directly to the office this morning." The perky girl appeared eager and self-assured as if the job was a done deal.

"I'm sorry, but Mr. Redmond isn't in at the moment." She smiled an apology. "You can leave your résumé with me, and I'll see he gets it the moment he returns."

"I can wait." The young girl walked over to the sofa, her application clutched in her right hand next to her body as if it were a top-secret document.

"I'm sorry. Mr. Redmond won't be back until late this afternoon. He's meeting with a client. Can I schedule an appointment for you?"

The girl stopped short of sitting. "Great. So what about this afternoon?"

The girl was desperate, persistent, and obvious. And was chewing gum. This applicant had no chance in hell of getting the job.

"Have a seat while I get Mr. Redmond's calendar. I'll be right back."

She rushed to Mr. Redmond's office and stopped in the doorway. His office wasn't as plush as she expected, but it was orderly and efficient to a fault. She quickly walked around his desk, looked for and found a monthly planner spread open on the left-hand corner. Several folders she assumed belonged to other applicants were neatly stacked in the lower corner. If she was going to arrange appointments for this girl, she might as well arrange interviews for the others, as well. She lifted the folders along with the schedule book and dashed back to the front room. The girl was ensconced on the sofa, a long slender leg bouncing nervously over her right leg, her gauzy skirt flapping above her knees.

She returned to her desk, laid the folders to the side, and studied the planner, ignoring the girl who was now hovering over her shoulder waiting for an appointment date.

"I see Mr. Redmond doesn't have openings until tomorrow afternoon between three and five. He'll need a half hour for the interview. Is there a time that would work for you?"

"Well, I have an appointment for my nails at two thirty, so I might be a little late if I came at three. And I promised my friend I'd be at her place at four thirty so we could go shopping."

"Okay, what about the next day? He has the

morning free. Is morning a better time for you?"

"Not too early. How about ten thirty? I could be here at ten thirty after my toning class."

"I'll pencil you in for ten thirty. I'm assuming your contact information is in your file if we need to get in touch with you in case Mr. Redmond needs to postpone the interview."

She didn't know anything about Mr. Redmond's schedule other than what was written on his calendar. The page in front of her was practically blank.

"Yes, everything is in there. Bethany went over it with me."

She couldn't wait to meet Bethany. It was obvious she'd more than likely have to be vetted by Mr. Redmond's sister, too, if she hoped to be officially considered for this position.

She stood, hoping the applicant, who was twirling a long bleached-blonde strand of hair between slender fingers and her long, blood-red fingernails, would get the point and realize their conversation was at an end. She glanced at the name on the folder.

"Thanks for coming in, Ms. Knight." She circled the desk and extended her hand. "It was a pleasure meeting you. I'll see Mr. Redmond gets your résumé the minute he returns."

"Oh, oh, yes. You're welcome." Ms. Knight stood, snapped her gum, and accepted Nora's hand. "I'll see you day after tomorrow. Thank you so much."

She exhaled the minute Tiffany Knight closed the door on her way out. If the young girl came to the interview chewing gum, Nora knew the girl didn't stand a chance of being hired.

She took the liberty to read through the remaining

files, and without meaning to, compared them to her own credentials. Ms. Knight's and the other two contenders were milquetoast compared to her own credentials, but the third applicant was slightly more qualified. Consulting Mr. Redmond's calendar, Nora continued to schedule appointments for the remaining three applicants and penciled in the information on his calendar.

Crap. She was going to have to check back in with the employment agency and see if they had any other positions available in her line of work.

The phone rang, jarring her from her contemplations. She stared at the phone as if it were ready to bite. Her mind cleared, refocused, and she picked up the receiver. "Redmond's Marine Resources Management."

"This is Coleman Baker at McClintock and McClintock Lobster Fisheries. May I speak to Gavin, please?"

"I'm sorry, Mr. Redmond isn't in at the moment. Can I take a message?"

"Yes. Tell him I've had to move our meeting to two o'clock this afternoon."

"I'll be sure he gets the message."

Nora hadn't expected to be personally involved with the McClintocks. She wasn't ready to come face to face, or even over the phone, with Sebastian's family. She knew she couldn't hide forever. Mr. Redmond was more than likely going to hire one of the applicants she'd scheduled an interview for, so the chance of meeting any of the McClintocks was a moot point.

Her connection to the McClintock family wasn't what one would call cordial. Despite her having had an affair with their son, Sebastian, she'd been summoned to the reading of his will only to discover he had set up a bank account in her name. Information he had kept to himself. Of course, his name was also on the account, and he'd had no intention of letting her know about it. So when Günther Jordan, the McClintocks' lawyer, announced she was the recipient of a large sum of money, she was shocked speechless. As was Sebastian's mother, Eugenia, and Sebastian's wife, Juelle. After Eugenia's less-than-understanding demeanor, throwing a fit worse than Nora had thrown at the cemetery, she had refused the money. But Mr. Jordan stated the money was rightfully hers and therefore the McClintocks had no legal right to it. To her, it was tainted money. If anyone had the "right" to the money, it should have been Juelle, if for no other reason than for Juelle's baby.

She had stormed out of Mr. Jordan's office before she made a bigger fool of herself. Her mind a blank, she drove back home, only to realize the "home" she lived in wasn't hers. It belonged to Sebastian. When Mr. Jordan called later in the day, she'd already decided to donate the money to one of the McClintocks' funds, namely the local Wounded Veteran's Association Fund.

Sebastian's mother, Eugenia McClintock, had looked down her nose at her, thrown a fit, and called her a few unsavory names. The woman had looked as if she were about to have a heart attack. But then, the look on the old woman's face when she refused the money had been priceless. Thankfully Mr. Jordan was a kind man and had stepped in, taken over, and administered the transfer without her having to deal with Eugenia McClintock. Or any of the McClintocks for that matter.

Now, not for the first time over the past year, she contemplated the wisdom of turning the entire amount over to the McClintocks' local Wounded Veteran's Association Fund. She sure could use some of the money. Still, it wasn't her money. She hadn't earned a single dime and wanted no part of it.

Had she been too hasty?

Chapter Three

"What do you mean you're already on the job this morning? You just applied. Don't tell me you were hired on the spot?"

"It's temporary, Jackie. Mr. Redmond was in a fix. His current hire bailed on him this morning. He's expecting an important call and needed someone to sit in the office while he was out."

"I knew it. I knew once he took a look at you and reviewed your awesome résumé, he'd hire you on the spot."

"I don't want to be hired for my looks. You know better. Besides, you have some explaining to do. You should have filled me in last night after you told me who the assistant coach was. You knew I had an appointment with him today."

"Well, technically I didn't know your interview would be with him. What did you think of him?"

She wasn't about to tell Jackie that up close and personal Gavin Redmond was an Adonis—a Greek god. A man with a body to make most females' hearts race the minute he appeared in their crosshairs. She wondered what he would look like in a wet suit and scuba gear.

"I was a bit intimated by the way he stood in the alcove entryway. I almost turned around and walked out."

His dark hair had hugged his ears, not to mention his slacks had hugged his hips. And his piercing ocean-blue eyes had stopped her in her tracks.

"OMG, Nora, the two of you would make a perfect couple. I can imagine the hearts you would be breaking if you walked down the street together. You with your blonde-bombshell, amazing looks and him a tall, dark Adonis. I can picture it," Jackie gushed over the phone.

"Not gonna happen, Jackie. I'm not looking for another tall, dark, handsome man. I've sworn off all men. I need to concentrate on getting my life back in order. Besides, I went through the applicants' résumés I found on his desk and scheduled each of them an appointment. Other than the one who walked in this morning snapping gum, which he professes to hate, one applicant is better qualified than I am. So my appointment is a moot point."

"You scheduled their appointments? What is the matter with you?" Jackie chastised. "You should have called them and told them the position was filled."

"I don't have the job. And again, Jackie, that's not who I am. I don't want to be hired for my looks. As you know, I have a perfectly well-earned degree, a functioning mind, and moral ethics. They've all been readjusted and put back in place. One slipup with Sebastian. Only one. I learned my lesson. My eyes are wide open. I won't be falling for any good-looking Lotharios, including Mr. Gavin Redmond."

"Too bad. Sounds like he's an intriguing guy. I know he's a great assistant coach. So what time are we meeting for lunch? We have a lot to talk about."

"You're darn right we have a lot to talk about. But about lunch today, I have to cancel." She held her breath. She didn't want to tell Jackie Mr. Redmond had invited her to lunch for an interview. Jackie would want to know every last detail. However, it wasn't a conversation she intended to have with her friend.

"Oh, no! What happened? I was looking forward to a relaxing meal while the boys are in school."

She hesitated. There was no getting around sharing this with Jackie. She'd find out sooner rather than later, anyway.

"Mr. Redmond is taking me to lunch to interview me when he returns. I accepted, seeing as it was the least he could do after putting me on the spot and asking me to watch the office for him this morning."

"Honey, the job is yours. I guarantee it!"

She didn't like Jackie's gleeful chuckle coming over the phone.

"Girlfriend, you are coming over for dinner tonight. No arguments." Jackie's tone was too hopeful. "I want details. No holding back. Six o'clock. You'd better be here, or I'm coming looking for you. And I know where you live."

"I've gotta go, Jackie. The office phone is ringing, and it might be Mr. Redmond's important call."

"Six o'clock."

She gave in. "Okay. Six o'clock."

****

Gavin climbed the ladder slung over the side of the fishing boat, clasped his left hand on the deck railing, lifted his goggles over his head, and shook the water off his hair.

"Eric. Did I get any calls while I was down below? I'm waiting on one from the Marine Consultant Society."

"Nope. But we are out a ways, and the reception has been sporadic lately."

He hoped he hadn't made a mistake coercing Nora Spears into manning the office this morning. He didn't need another ditzy blonde at the office—or in his life. Bethany had tried to fix him up with a few, including sending him potential office assistants who couldn't add and subtract, let alone spell worth a damn, and it drove him crazy. They wrongfully assumed autocorrect fixed their lack of spelling and editing skills. He needed someone who was competent, had initiative, and was honest to a fault. What he didn't need was some simpering sexpot who was after the bottom line, regardless of who they hurt along the way. Hell, if Ms. Spears had any smarts, she would have already left and locked the door behind her, as he'd suggested.

"What'd you find down there? Anything suspicious?"

Eric gave Gavin a hand as he hefted his legs over the edge of the boat. Water puddled on the deck.

"No. It's still a puzzle. I did snag a few plants, enough sediment to fill a vial, and an unusual shell for this area." He slipped out of his flippers, careful not to slide as he stepped to the side and sat on the long wooden bench lining the rails. "I'll take them back to the lab and see what I can find. Are you sure there has been no suspicious activity in the area over the past month? Something to indicate a drop in catch?"

"Nothing obvious," Eric confirmed.

"I hope you put sufficient ice in the cooler to last until we get back to shore." He took his own catch from the pouches he'd attached to his hips and handed them to Eric.

Eric did his bidding and then signaled to Al, who was at the helm ready to cast off.

"We've been keeping a sharp eye on things again this past week. If anything's been going on previously, we aren't aware of it," Eric said. "We basically attributed it to all the uproar we've been hearing about global warming and the backwash from the cruise ships leaching into the water."

"I think it's something more. But once I get back and check out these samples, I'll have a better idea of what's going on. The nets don't look tampered with, but you never know. Give me a minute to get out of these diving togs, and then we can relax before we get back to shore."

"I've prepared a snack and brew in the cabin below," Eric said. "I'll bring it on deck so we can enjoy the wide-open waters while the sun is high and the air temperate."

Gavin consulted his watch. He had a luncheon date. The more he thought about Ms. Nora Spears, the more he didn't want to be late. He hoped she was still there, waiting for his return. It had been one hell of a long time since someone waited for his return from sea. It was a warm and comforting feeling, one he really shouldn't be contemplating. He shook his head. He'd been below too long. His mind was awash from the pressures of the deep. It was the only excuse he could come up with at the moment.

He had no time for such frivolous emotions.

****

The door was unlocked when he walked in to find an empty office. Good God! She'd left and didn't have the smarts to lock the door as he'd instructed? And she'd left the lights on, as well as the computer, and the... Wait a minute, was someone singing in the kitchen? He didn't hear any music. The woman probably had ear buds stuck in her head. He checked his watch. Eleven thirty. Had his office assistant decided to return after all?

He tromped toward the alcove only to have someone round the corner and bump into him. A warm, soft, lush body landed against his chest. Definitely not his usual office assistant. He was shocked to discover Nora Spears' body, a head shorter than him, fit in his arms perfectly. She smelled of hazelnut, sugar, and sea mist. He drank in her scent and smiled as her arms grasped him for support.

"Oh, I'm sorry. I didn't hear you come in."

Her voice muffled in his chest rippled clear to his lower man parts. His smile turned into a groan.

She tipped her head toward his face, stepped out of his arms, and walked around him. He felt the loss of heat and took a moment to shed the sensual pull her touch invoked. He quickly pulled himself back under control and followed her to her desk.

"Coleman Baker called and rescheduled your appointment for two o'clock this afternoon," she said, handing him a sticky note. "Your office assistant, Ms. Shelby, called to say she wasn't going to be in at all today due to a family matter. Oh, and a Ms. Tiffani Knight stopped by. Apparently your sister sent her to see you. She has an appointment for Friday, but you aren't going to like her. She chews gum."

"Call her and tell her the job has been filled."

"Excuse me? You should at least give her the time of day."

"Not gonna happen."

"Well then, I took the liberty to arrange a few more interviews for you. Ms. Shelby says her family situation will take her away from the office for an extended period of time. I assumed you'd want to get the interviews arranged as soon as possible. I checked your monthly planner, and there didn't appear to be anything scheduled the next two days. I arranged appointments for half-hour intervals starting tomorrow."

"What else did you do while I was away from the office?" He cleared his throat, stuffed his hands in his pockets, and had no control over the smile that surfaced as he watched her circle her desk and pick up another note pad with the list of interviews.

"I took a few messages. The consultants you wanted to hear from called a few minutes ago. They had nothing to report and needed another week. Said they'd get back to you next Friday. Oh, and your sister called. Was surprised to learn I was filling in, and wanted you to call her as soon as you returned."

She handed him more sticky notes. He accepted without looking at them and shoved them in his pocket.

"Are you ready to go to lunch?"

Her head snapped up in disbelief. "It's really not necessary. I read the applicants' résumés, and a Mrs. Armstrong appears to be the most qualified."

"Nevertheless, I promised lunch and an interview. I'm starved. Being on the ocean all morning always gives me an appetite. Get your things."

"If you're sure. I could use a bite to eat."

"Yes, I'm sure." Her efficiency was a surprise and a welcome relief.

"Where shall I meet you?" she asked, biting her

lower lip.

He watched her straighten the desk, pull out the bottom drawer, and retrieve her purse.

"Mariner's Fish Fry, over in Lobster Cove."

"What about right here at Bar Harbor's docks? I understand they do a delicious lobster melt."

"I'll be able to make the two o'clock meeting with Coleman Baker at McClintock's Fisheries if we lunch at Mariner's. It's not far from there. Let me grab the files from my office while you take care of things here. I won't be but a minute."

He'd already decided to hire Nora Spears the minute he walked in, and she'd reported she'd organized his life for the next three days without being told to do so. Initiative? The woman had it in spades. She might be young and blonde, but she had already proven she had a good head on her shoulders. She didn't chew gum. And she hadn't had ear buds plugged into her ears, after all. Her singing voice was as melodic without music as her speech. Pleasant. Soothing. It was a welcome relief. He was thoroughly sick of having to deal with young women whose high-pitched, whiny, sugary-sweet voices were meant to be a turn-on but weren't.

He had to have a talk with his sister.

He shuddered, retrieved the files from the cabinet, and strode from his office. Nora Spears was waiting at the entrance, the lights off, and the answering machine light on. Efficient. What had he ever done to deserve to have her land on his doorstep looking for a job?

"I'll meet you at Mariner's in twenty."

Nora slung her purse over her shoulder and walked out the door, leaving him to shut and lock the office. He watched, mesmerized, as she walked down the street, rounded the corner, and disappeared. Had he made the biggest mistake of his business career hiring her on the spot?

****

Whew! The man was intense. The drive to Lobster Cove would be a short reprieve from Gavin Redmond's magnetic good looks and personality, and give her time to prepare for said interview. But Mariner's? It was the last place she wanted to have lunch with him or anyone. Roark and Dawn Sullivan owned Mariner's. Their daughter, Katelyn Logan, was Juelle McClintock's best friend. After the spectacular spectacle she'd made of herself in front of all of them at Sebastian's burial, she wasn't ready to face them ever again. She should have declined his lunch invitation. The interview part was no longer necessary. If he had any sense, he would hire the applicant who had more experience.

Lobster Cove was a quaint, cozy town, and she loved the way it hugged the seashore. It was a town built on shipping, fishing, and many Irish immigrants. Sebastian's family had been one of many to come ashore back in the day. Her heart picked up a rapid beat, remembering his dark good looks, his sexy body, and the warm affection he'd had for her. She'd loved him. Was going to marry him and share a happy-ever-after. He'd convinced her his marriage to Juelle was a mistake from the beginning. They'd had a fling in college, he said. If Juelle hadn't gotten pregnant, he never would have married her.

She believed him.

She shouldn't have. He'd played her. He might have opened a banking account in her name, paid her

35

rent, and treated her like a princess, but he cheated on her with a younger girl who lived on the other side of the island, like he'd cheated on his wife. She hadn't found out until months after his funeral. And now, she was about to face Lobster Cove residents and those whose lives Sebastian had impacted.

Mariner's parking lot was crowded when she pulled in behind Gavin Redmond's car. She swung her small Volvo behind the restaurant overlooking the bay. An assortment of colorful, licensed lobster buoys hung along the roof's edge. Old wooden lobster traps and nets were stacked against the building, and an old, short, squatty lighthouse overlooking the bay was the establishment's main focal point. Gavin met her as she exited her vehicle.

"Although it's a lovely day and sitting on the back deck would be pleasant," he greeted her, "I suggest we go in the front entrance and find a more private booth inside."

She agreed and didn't resist when he took her arm and led her to the front of the building. His touch was intimate, sending a jolt of warm sensations straight to her inner core. She walked past people milling under the green canopy entrance, their stares had her neck and cheeks burning. She hadn't realized she'd been holding her breath until he released her to open the door. The coolness of the interior and the dim lighting as they entered was a relief. She exhaled, her lungs aching from the pressure of holding her breath.

Dawn Sullivan, Katelyn's mother, greeted them. Nora wanted to turn tail, run, and leave Gavin Redmond to think what he wanted. She didn't need Lobster Cove residents looking down their noses at her even more than they did already.

"Nora. What a surprise." The woman's tone walked the line at being cordial. She knew it wasn't easy for Mrs. Sullivan to be pleasant, but then this encounter wasn't exactly a piece of cake for her, either.

"Mrs. Sullivan." She nodded and shuffled closer to Gavin's side, hoping he would take the hint, be the gentleman he obviously was, and jump into the conversation to take the attention away from her. From the corner of her eye, she watched as he assessed the situation in a flash.

His arm came around her, pulled her against his warm, firm, secure body, and he gave Mrs. Sullivan a sensual, telling smile. "We'd like a private booth if you have one, please. The lady and I have private business to discuss and don't want to be disturbed. A bottle of your finest wine would be lovely. Thank you."

"Oh. Yes. Certainly, Mr. Redman." Mrs. Sullivan's face became contrite and turned a vivid pink. "I'll get Aimee to seat you right away."

As bright as Mrs. Sullivan's face had become, hers grew equally as heated at the intimacy Gavin Redmond had implied. Thankfully the woman turned to get Aimee Hart's attention and didn't witness her embarrassment. Before she had a chance to step from Gavin's arms, he released her, leaned over, and whispered in her ear. An intimate action to those watching, no doubt.

"I assume you have some history here? You should have said something. We could have lunched elsewhere."

His breath tickled the hairs on her neck. She held her breath and turned to look into his eyes, the depths of which swallowed her whole.

A big mistake.

Momentarily mesmerized, she mentally shook herself and stepped aside. "Thanks. But I'm fine."

She wasn't. She'd give anything to escape and never come back.

"Come right this way." Aimee's smile was contagious, however, and helped put her at ease.

The young girl led them to a windowless booth in the far corner. As soon as Nora slid in on the red padded vinyl seat across from Gavin, they were handed laminated menus.

"I'm Aimee, and I'll be your waitress today. I know you already ordered wine, but if I can get you anything else, let me know."

"Two ice waters with lemon, please," Gavin said.

"You got it."

Aimee sauntered away, the bright, engaging smile still on her face. Apparently the waitress either didn't know who she was or hadn't heard the gossip. Or didn't care.

"So you want to tell me what that was all about?" Gavin didn't bother to open the menu before he started interrogating her.

"Nothing to tell. History under the bridge, over the dam. Whatever."

"Obviously not pleasant history."

"Let's say I'm not well liked by this town's esteemed citizens. Especially the McClintocks and their friends. So you might want to reconsider interviewing me."

"Let's order first."

Her appetite fled. The man wasn't listening. Was

he being pigheaded and obtuse on purpose? No way was she going to be an asset to his company if he was dealing with the McClintocks. Juelle and her new husband, as far as she knew, still owned the company. And Mr. Redmond had a meeting with their company's manager following lunch. Should she tell him about her ill-fated connection to the McClintocks?

Aimee returned with wine before they could continue the conversation. The wine was poured, and they placed their order. When the waitress left, Gavin Redmond lifted his glass for a toast. Nora lifted her glass to his, as expected, but was thrown for a loop when he made the toast.

"To a new joint venture. Welcome to Redmond's Marine Life Resource Management." He clicked her glass and took a deep swallow.

She set her glass on the table and stared at him, speechless. He raised his eyebrow in question and waited.

"You didn't even interview me. And knowing I have bad karma in Lobster Cove, with equally bad karma with the McClintocks, your main client, why would you consider hiring me without researching my background?"

"Drink up. I know all I need to know. The minute I saw you this morning, you had the job."

"Wait a minute. You hired me because of my looks?"

"Well, that and the fact my sister Bethany hadn't gotten to you first."

She wasn't sure she wanted to meet Bethany. Him wanting to hire her because of her looks brought back all her experiences growing up. At first, her looks had been an asset, but it didn't take long once she hit her teens to finally understand they could also be a thorn in her behind. Boys might have flocked to her, but girls were jealous and could be mean spirited. Girls became her friend only because boys congregated around her. Keeping a true friend was as hard as finding one in the first place. And boys lost interest the minute they discovered they couldn't get to first base with her on their first date. Her so-called "friends" were on hand to soothe her dates' battered egos when she turned them down. And there had been many girls who stood in line.

No, she didn't want to be hired on looks alone. She didn't want Gavin Redmond to show interest in her due to her looks. She had hoped he would see beyond her outward appearance and discover she had a brain—and feelings.

"I didn't say I'd take the job. Hiring me on the basis of my looks doesn't bode well for my employment. I've dealt with difficult people in the workplace before, and I was hoping to get past the superficial." And beyond, if it came to that. Even if it wasn't in the workforce, her landlord Chuck's sexual innuendoes was one more reason she needed to vacate her apartment, sooner rather than later.

"If you mean 'sexually' difficult people, you don't have to worry. I was a happily married man until two years ago when my wife was diagnosed with cancer. She died shortly thereafter. I'm not looking for a relationship, although my sister considers I should be. I'm not. So now we've gotten that out of the way, accept the position and drink up."

"We haven't discussed my responsibilities, my hours, and my pay, as well as additional benefits. Not to mention my qualifications."

"If you insist." He set his glass on the table and folded his hands next to it. "The responsibilities are varied—between an office assistant's and an accountant's duties. It includes some travel. Hours can also vary but are mostly eight thirty in the morning until five in the afternoon, Monday through Friday, unless we are working on a special project. Time off is negotiable, and benefits include health insurance and retirement."

"What about pay?" The job itself sounded as if she would be on call twenty-four seven. Thankfully her schedule was accommodating, and she had no other responsibilities holding her back from working those hours. But she needed a salary to allow her to remain in her current apartment until she could find something more suitable.

"Ah, yes, that reminds me. Here is a check for this morning's hours."

Her eyes rounded when she saw the amount. "This is too much for four hours of work."

"Yes, but you saved my ass this morning, so it is well worth every penny, as they say."

He named an hourly rate with time and a half for overtime, doubled if he needed her to work weekends. It was so tempting she almost accepted it on the spot. But was this the right job for her?

"I'd feel more comfortable if you interviewed the other applicants and actually read my application before you made a decision."

"After your performance this morning, I'm confident I've made the right choice. You're self-motivated. It goes a long way in any company. I need someone to take charge the way you did this morning, scheduling appointments."

He lifted his wine glass and held it across the table, waiting for her to do the same.

"By the way," he continued, "you can call every applicant and tell each one the job has been filled."

"But I haven't accepted."

Aimee Hart arrived with their meal and placed the steaming shrimp scampi rice dish in front of them. The heaven-sent aroma made her stomach rumble. She reached for her wine glass and chugged half the contents without thinking. She liked wine, but she wasn't a heavy drinker. But darn the man, she needed something to calm the chaotic ramblings coursing through her system. She didn't like the frown on Gavin Redmond's face as he refilled her glass as soon as she set it down. He was abrupt, assuming, and handsome as sin.

Damn it, she didn't want to be hired for her looks. Okay, so he liked initiative, if he was to be believed. But how could she refuse the generous salary?

"What if I take the job temporarily and see how things go? You can let me go if I don't work out to your satisfaction, and I'll quit if I'm in over my head."

"Deal." He raised his glass across the table again.

This time, after clinking their glasses together, she sipped the wine, letting the sweet essence of the grape linger on her tongue before digging in to her meal.

Good Lord! I'm so over my head already.

Chapter Four

"Yes! I knew you'd land the job." Jackie pumped her fist in the air.

Nora leaned back in the blue Adirondack chair in Jackie's backyard and shook her head. Chunks of ice clinked in her lemonade as she took a long sip. The cold liquid soothed her insides.

"Honey, you can move forward with your life and forget all about Sebastian McClintock," Jackie continued.

"It's hard to forget. And I'm not looking for another man to take his place. Lesson learned. I need to concentrate on this job. And, as far as working for Mr. Redmond for one day, I can tell it's going to be a good fit. He spends a lot of time away from the office. When he is there, he's most likely going to be in his lab."

"What about all those interviews you set up?"

"I felt terrible having to call everyone to notify them the job had been filled," she said, lifting her glass and jiggling the ice in the lemonade before taking a drink and draining her glass. "I waited until an hour before I left for the day to make the calls. Cowardly of me, I know. But I couldn't get in touch with the young girl who came in today. She isn't due in until Friday, so I'll call her tomorrow."

"What about the sister?"

"Bethany? Not looking forward to meeting her.

Sounds as if she's judgmental or looking for someone to have a fling with her brother."

Jackie shifted in her seat, reached for the glass pitcher of lemonade, and poured them each a refill.

"What? What aren't you telling me, Jackie? Come on, out with it."

"Well, rumor has it he's sworn off women after his wife died of cancer. Guess he was so heartbroken because he wasn't there for her when she needed him. Supposedly he's not interested in forming another relationship. He's too busy getting the family business back up and running."

"That explains why his sister seems to be throwing young, sexy girls his way. Trust me, I'm not looking for a relationship anytime soon, either. I need to concentrate on finding another place to live, getting my life back in order, and starting my own business. This job is only temporary and will help me finance my long-time dream."

"Will you have enough to cover this month's rent so you won't be left stranded on the streets? You know you can move in with us temporarily."

"Thanks, but there is no way I am going to take advantage of our friendship. Besides, Mr. Redmond gave me a check to cover this morning's hours. I guess he thought I was going to either refuse working for him, and this was an incentive to encourage me to accept his offer, or he was going to tell me to look for another job. As far as I'm concerned, it was more than enough to cover an entire day's work. So of course, I agreed to work in the afternoon, too. It'll help cover this month's rent, so you're off the hook with your offer. Which I appreciate, by the way. But I'm going to look for a cheaper place as soon as possible. Someplace that won't remind me of Sebastian—and the disaster our relationship turned out to be. I should have found something sooner, I know. But honestly, I didn't know how to let go."

"Good to hear you finally have. It's about time."

"I'm going to call the realtor tomorrow and see what's available. I'm going to pick up another newspaper tonight and see what they have listed."

A sudden clash of doors banging open and feet skittering down the steps into the backyard ended Nora and Jackie's private conversation. She smiled as Jackie's two boys ran into the yard, kicking a soccer ball to each other. Jackie's husband, Brad, tall, blond, and wearing a red and white Hawaiian shirt and matching shorts, followed carrying a large platter filled with hamburgers ready for the grill.

"Dinner will be ready in about twenty minutes," he announced.

"That's my signal to start getting the tableware and salads on the table."

"I'll help." She jumped from her chair and followed Jackie into the house, marveling at the domestic scene surrounding her. Would she ever experience a fulfilling home life like Jackie's? She had hoped and dreamed once she and Sebastian were married, they would have children, raise a family. Those dreams had washed away soon after she'd discovered he and Juelle had a child. A child he didn't seem to want. She had started to realize their relationship wasn't going anywhere, but had ignored all the signs.

****

The meeting with Coleman Baker had gone better than Gavin expected. Coleman had run him through the main points of the business.

"We're a viable company," Coleman assured him. "Although, it was a bit iffy after Mr. McClintock Senior died. Business had begun to improve rapidly, and then all of a sudden, it went downhill just as rapidly under Sebastian McClintock's leadership. How about I show you around, meet a couple of our men? It will give you a broader idea of our operations. Maybe as an outsider, you'll be able to spot something we haven't put our fingers on yet."

Coleman switched off a few controls, grabbed a set of keys, and escorted him out into the hallway before locking the door behind them.

"It's never a good idea to leave expensive equipment and files unattended, especially after everything that's been going on around here. Follow me."

Coleman led him down a narrow corridor where he opened a door leading into a long warehouse. Large aerated tanks lined both sides of the spacious room. The temperature was cool, the scent of seawater and marine life concentrated.

"This is our holding facility. We've upgraded our systems to chill the water temperature to thirty-six degrees in the tanks. As you know, this allows for better quality and taste, and it locks in the freshness. We have a water filtration system to simulate the lobsters' natural environs, which helps maintain their freshness before we ship them, as well as during shipment."

Coleman called to a man leaning over one of the tanks at the far end of the building. "Jim. Got a minute?"

A man with a five o'clock shadow, looking to be about in his fifties, looked up and then ambled over.

"This is Jim Sherman, our tank room manager. He oversees the grading process. This is Gavin Redmond, doing some research on the area fisheries."

"Pleased to meet you." Gavin shook Jim's hand, aware Coleman didn't divulge the real reason he was there.

"Gavin is here to find out a bit about our operation."

"Well, we have a quality control team. Five of the most experienced lobster men in town and a few newly hired hands who seem to know what they're doing. Hard to explain the control process, but experience is key. These men know a thing or two about lobsters. They've been at it a long time. The McClintocks are lucky to have them."

Gavin wasn't so sure about the luck, but he kept up a personable commentary with the men as they inspected the tanks, and then he stepped outside onto the pier to check out the fleet. The McClintock Fisheries had two trawlers tied up at the pier at the moment. But harbor life thrived, and the area was afloat with kayaks, sailboats, and in the distance, a cruise ship tendering in passengers near Bar Harbor. Not surprising, Pier Two, across the way, was a beehive of activity with tourists and locals visiting the vendors and carts lined up along the midway for the evening crowd.

"Most of our fleet left early this morning and haven't returned yet. We maintain a fleet of fifteen," Coleman stated. "Our captains are experienced and dependable, and our trawlers are equipped with the latest technology. We employ a few private fishermen during our busy season. The McClintocks have secured the rights to several of the fishing areas."

"Impressive."

After returning to the warehouse, Coleman confided in him that although the McClintock business was holding their financial status steady, they'd barely been able to supply their clients with an ample amount of requested fresh catch the past month. The single lead Gavin could provide was that it appeared their traps and nets weren't the only ones being targeted. Although the licensed area north of the McClintock traps was also being sabotaged, they hadn't been as hard hit. He had found no chemical imbalances in any of the tests he had taken, which meant the ocean floor wasn't being damaged and didn't account for the dwindling number of lobsters.

After he returned home later that evening, Gavin checked his test results and put in a call to Coleman with the lab reports. He'd barely had time to sit down at the table to eat when his front door swung open and a gust of fresh air whooshed through the foyer.

"Gavin! What's going on?" Bethany demanded. "I've had two weepy applicants call me, demanding to know why their appointments were suddenly cancelled."

"Hi, Beth. Come on in, why don't you?" He stepped aside to let his sister enter the large foyer. The old cottage on Eden Street, once his grandparents', now his, held memories from a childhood both he and his sister shared. But having her drop by unannounced today could only mean one thing. She'd found out he'd hired someone she hadn't scrutinized first.

"What brings you here tonight? As if I can't guess. You might as well join me for dinner. I was about to sit down."

"What a greeting." She kissed him on the cheek and made her way to the dining room.

"I'm eating in the kitchen tonight. I'm afraid it's simply pizza and a salad. It's been a busy day." His meeting with Coleman Baker sitting at the top of his list.

"So I gather." Bethany headed to the kitchen, sat at the circular table, and helped herself to a slice of pizza waiting in the open box.

He dished out salad from the bowl on the counter and poured soft drinks before he joined her at the table. "So what do I owe the honor of this visit?"

"This woman you hired? Why did you let her arbitrarily dismiss the others I already pre-interviewed for you?"

"Girls. They were all young girls."

"Girls I've already interviewed for you. They were all qualified."

"They were all too young and inexperienced. Listen, Beth, I'm not looking for a relationship, especially some young blonde bimbo who has one thing in mind. I'm not interested in any of them. And I'm not interested in an office affair."

"I want you to be happy, Gav. You should see how you've moped about these last two years. Even Mother agrees. It's time to move on."

He rolled his pizza and took a bite, the cheese stretching between the crust and his teeth. He pulled on it, chewed, and swallowed.

"I'll be happy when I'm happy. In the meantime,

hoping to fix me up with one or more of these girls isn't going to work. I need to concentrate on continuing to get this business back in shape. And solve the McClintock case."

"And when will you be satisfied the business is back in shape? Huh? When will that be? We're all worried about you."

"Yes, well, just because Mom has moved on, and you're happily married to Ed, doesn't mean I have to have a woman in my life to be happy, too. I certainly don't want someone young enough to be my daughter."

"They aren't that young. And you aren't that old."

"Let it go, Bethany. I'm not in the market."

"So tell me all about this new woman you hired on the spot. What, is she fifty, pudgy, and has salt and pepper hair?"

He gave her a piercing glance, a gaze he realized didn't faze her in the least. He took another bite of pizza, washed it down with his soft drink, and cleared his throat.

"Are you more upset you didn't get to vet her first? Or the fact you don't know anything about her looks? For your information, she is a few years younger than me, about your age, is blonde, and is a beautiful, single woman. But I am not interested in her as a fling or a relationship. She's efficient, self-motivated, and actually insisted I hire one of the other applicants."

"Really? Then why didn't you hire one of the other applicants instead?"

Good question. He was still trying to figure that one out. And he wasn't about to share his knowledge of Nora Spears' connection to the McClintocks.

"She didn't get all demure or fawn all over me. She

took control at a moment's notice and took the initiative to actually do some work while I was out of the office. I haven't been disappointed so far."

"So far? It's only been one day, for goodness' sake."

"Are you going to eat the last piece of pizza?"

"You're evading my question."

"It wasn't a question. Eat your salad."

"You're impossible."

"So I've been told. Was there another reason you stopped by tonight?"

"Yes. Mom called. Wanted to make sure you were going to attend the memorial for the fallen vets at the Lobster Cove annual Memorial Day celebration, you being a vet and all. Dad is being honored post mortem, too."

"I'll be there."

"In uniform?"

"Don't push it, sis. It's been a few years. I'm pretty sure the uniform is a bit snug."

"You aren't out of shape, Gav. Try it on. Mom would be proud. So would Dad."

"We'll see."

His Air Force blues still hung in the closet. After serving tours in Iraq and Afghanistan, he'd had enough destruction of human lives. His father had wanted him to be a Navy SEAL like him, but the closest he came was becoming a marine biologist when he left the armed forces. Some might consider it a cop-out—to him it still amounted to a search and rescue operation— whether marine life or human life, men's livelihoods relied on his findings.

He opened his bedroom closet after Bethany left,

pulled his uniform from the far reaches behind the suits, and stared at it. He'd been proud to serve his country, was still moved whenever he remembered the many lives he and his men had saved. He contemplated the men he hadn't been able to save and put the uniform back in the closet. He'd show up and do his part, even though he didn't need the recognition. He hadn't served his country to be considered a hero. He might have managed a minor bullet scratch to his leg, but if anyone was a hero, it was his wife. Battling cancer, keeping it to herself for so long, not wanting him to know, knowing he'd quit the military to look after her. And she had been right. He wished he had quit sooner and had been able to spend more time with her—time to take care of her when she'd needed him the most.

****

Nora read over the instructions Gavin had left on her desk early the next morning. His note said he would be in the lab until noon and didn't want to be interrupted unless a major emergency developed. She wasn't sure what he considered a major emergency, but she'd have to play it by ear. She logged into the email system and retrieved the directions for finding all the security codes, passwords to files, clients' email addresses and phone numbers, and the combination to the safe in his office. Obviously he was an extremely confident and trusting man, or a careless one, if he trusted her with this information so soon after hiring her. Even Sebastian hadn't trusted her with the knowledge he'd set up an account at the bank in her name. She could only imagine what else he'd kept from her. Not for the first time, she wondered if he had been serious about divorcing Juelle.

On a sigh, she made her way to the alcove where the coffee machine's light blinked, waiting to be pressed. She popped a hazelnut coffee pod in the dispenser, a large cup underneath, and hit brew. The immediate nutty coffee aroma filled the room. She closed her eyes and let it seep into her senses. After adding sugar and a large dollop of creamy half and half, she took a hearty sip, letting the warm caffeine slide smoothly into her system. It would be mere minutes before the much-needed caffeine kicked in.

She rounded the alcove corner on her way back to her desk and stopped short. A tall woman who definitely had to be Gavin Redmond's sister stood in the entryway. The young woman had the same dark, piercing blue eyes as Gavin. Her dark auburn hair hung below her shoulders with long, wispy strands swept back behind her ears. She was as beautiful as Gavin was handsome. They both had high cheekbones and a well-defined long nose. Her full lips were covered with a deep rose shade of lip gloss, which matched her nail polish. Nora's own knock-off work dress of pale lavender felt limp and subdued in comparison to Gavin's sister's crisp blue denim shirtdress and matching navy braided belt.

"You must be Nora Spears, the new administrative accountant. I'm Bethany Hawthorn, Gavin's sister."

Nora placed her cup on a napkin on her desk and extended her hand to Bethany. "Nice to meet you."

Bethany didn't hesitate and shook her hand in a firm confident grip.

"I'm sorry, but your brother is in the lab this morning and asked not to be disturbed until noon. Can I give him a message?"

"No problem. I'll go back and give him the message myself. I'm sure he won't mind."

"Let me give him a call and let him know you're coming."

"Not necessary. I know my way." Bethany drifted through the alcove, waving her hand behind her. "Nice to meet you."

Nora lifted the phone and called through to the lab. It rang twice before Gavin answered.

"This better be an emergency." His tone was hassled.

She pictured him running his hand through his rich, dark hair. "If you call the fact that your sister is on her way to the lab as we speak, then yes, it's an emergency. I thought you'd want to know."

"Shit."

The phone banged in her ear. She felt sorry for Bethany when she arrived at Gavin's lab. It didn't sound as if things were going well with whatever he was working on.

She hung up, turned to the computer, and immersed herself with the Redmond accounts. Half an hour later, she heard Bethany in the kitchenette making herself a cup of coffee. Cup in hand, Bethany returned, sat on the sofa, and casually took a sip of the steaming brew. A mist of vanilla filled the tense space between them.

"So what's your story?" Bethany breathed as if she were exhaling a puff of smoke.

The woman's focus was meant to be intimidating, but Nora could be as direct and unflinching.

"I see you're as blunt as your brother."

"So I've been told. So how did you manage to

acquire this position in so short a time? What? A single minute?"

"Hardly. I worked an entire morning on-the-job training before he offered me the job."

"Not what I heard. I must admit, you actually look like someone I would have picked for Gav."

"I hope I haven't been given the job due to my looks. Just so you know, Bethany, I told your brother as much. And as long as we're being direct, you should know I insisted your brother hire someone you'd already vetted, whom I perceived to have more experience."

"Hmmm." Bethany lifted the cup to her lips and drew in half the contents before she settled it more securely in her lap, her brows raised. "I've heard stories about how you were involved with Sebastian McClintock."

"I'm sure you have. However, I'm not about to discuss my personal life, or all the sordid details, with you or anyone else. It's history. And no one else's business."

"Appreciate your candidness. Keeping it to yourself will go a long way in protecting the company's reputation. We don't need a scandal. In case you haven't figured it out yet, the McClintock's is Gavin's biggest client."

"Mr. Redmond and I have already discussed the matter. He hired me anyway."

"Bethany!" Gavin bellowed from the alcove doorway, a frown etched across his face, his eyebrows drawn. "Weren't you in a hurry to get to your appointment?"

Bethany stood and smiled at her brother. "Making

sure Ms. Spears has the stamina to deal with you and your clients on a daily basis. I'm convinced you're in good hands."

"I can assure you she has. And I am."

Bethany handed Gavin her empty cup. The smirk on her face didn't seem to intimidate him. He took the cup and shook his head. His chest heaved as he emitted a deep sigh.

"It's been a pleasure, Nora. No offense, no hard feelings?" Bethany waved as she walked toward the front entrance.

Nora rounded her desk, keeping her eyes on Bethany as Gavin's sister moved across the room. "None. Have a good day." She swung around to find Gavin's intense stare focused on her.

"I hope she wasn't off-putting. She can be quite intense." His words sounded like an apology.

"So I discovered. But I am a bit confused. I'm not sure whether she just vetted me and my past in order to determine if I have designs on you, or to save your company from the likes of me."

"She may be pushing for me to have a fling or two, but as I've already stated, that isn't going to happen. As far as the McClintocks being our major client is concerned, as much as my family professes it's a big deal, it's not going to make or break my business if I lose their account. I've recently picked up a couple other large accounts. And as you so articulately informed my sister, it's no one else's business but yours."

How long had he been standing there listening? Had he overheard the entire conversation? Did the McClintock case not have a bearing on his business as

Bethany had indicated?

"Thank you."

"No. Thank you for letting me know Bethany was on her way to the lab. It gave me time to make sure the specimens I'm working on wouldn't be contaminated, and so I could meet her at the door. She tends to walk around the lab to see what I'm working on if I don't catch her in time. My grandfather started the business. It's been in the family a long time, and she's hung out here a lot over the years. She thinks she has free reign where the business is concerned. Not to mention her husband is a cop, and she has it in her head she can help solve any mystery that comes along."

"I didn't know the protocol. Calling you seemed the right thing to do."

"It was. Thank you. Since I've been interrupted, this would be a perfect time to go over our clients' files and see if you have any questions about the accounting system. We can order lunch in from the lobster pound on the wharf. Save us from having to go out. I have a busy afternoon out on the bay ahead of me."

Chapter Five

Saturday morning, Jessica Martin, of the Jessica Martin Real Estate Agency, a young, strikingly beautiful businesswoman in her mid-twenties, met Nora and Jackie at the front door of a small bungalow hidden behind a row of tall pines. A flagstone sidewalk led from the dirt driveway to the front porch.

"Welcome, ladies. Come on in. I think you'll like this place. It's rather charming, and even though it's close to the park entrance, it's secluded and still close to town. There is a small backyard, already fenced in, but there are no other houses beyond. It's all woodland and is shaded most of the year. But it has a cozy fireplace in the front room, and the kitchen is small but adequate."

From the outside, it was ideal. Small, homey, and didn't appear to require much upkeep.

"It sounds lovely already." Nora smiled in anticipation. "I can't wait to see the inside."

She and Jackie followed Jessica inside and were immediately struck by the rustic, log-cabin look of the interior. A large brick fireplace covered an entire wall opposite the picture windows across the room that let in an abundance of sunshine from the east. She strode over to the window and peered out at a grand view of the bay.

"Wow, Nora. Plenty of room to snuggle up next to

the fire," Jackie said behind her. "How many bedrooms did you say there are?"

Leave it to Jackie to focus in on the bedrooms. Her friend's broad smile and sparkling eyes said it all and left her heart racing. She knew what Jackie was thinking, but there was no way she was considering entertaining men in her new home anytime soon. She needed to get her life in order. And hopefully set up her own home-based accounting business.

"Surprisingly, there are three, although one is rather small. I'm told it was used as a nursery at one time."

"Sounds as if it would make a perfect office," Nora said, giving Jackie a knowing look.

Jessica smiled and then led them down a narrow hallway toward the other bedrooms. The realtor was right. The smaller of the two rooms was perfect for a nursery, but it wasn't big enough for a desk and computer equipment, let alone a filing cabinet. The second room Jessica showed them, however, was ideal.

"The master room is down at this end." Jessica pointed farther down the hall. "I think you'll like it. It's big enough for a king-size bed, double dresser, and has a walk-in closet."

She thought it overindulgent for her needs. She wasn't into entertaining men. However, the minute she entered the room, thoughts of Gavin Redmond popped in her head. Decorated in warm shades of mauve, ceiling bordered with a rose-pattern trim, it was romantic.

"Wow, look at that," Jackie said, her tone suggestive, her smile wide. "How romantic."

Had Jackie read her mind? She ignored her friend.

Jackie was a romantic at heart. Her own fairytale happily-ever-afters were fractured, thanks to Sebastian.

"Is there a basement? Is it dry?" She changed the subject before Jackie could embarrass her further. If Jackie knew her mind had wandered in the same direction as hers, there'd be no end to the teasing. She didn't need her friend harassing her in front of the realtor.

"There is a small basement," Jessica said, friendly yet businesslike, leaving the bedroom area behind. "Follow me. The previous owner had a concrete floor put in and installed a washer and dryer. Other than the hot water heater and furnace, there isn't much room for more. Very compact."

After a thorough inspection of the "compact" basement, the trio returned to the sitting room.

"It's perfect," Nora assured Jessica. Her insides hummed at the thought of having a place of her own. A home she purchased with her own money, and not a house someone else owned, where they called the shots. But could she afford a home vs renting an apartment?

"Do you have other homes we can look at?" Jackie asked as if she were the one in the market for a new home. "It would be nice to have something to compare with this house, don't you agree, Jessica?"

"I do have something closer to Bar Harbor. It's small but a bit more upscale if that's what you're looking for. We haven't talked finances." She turned to Nora. "However, the owner of this house is willing to do a land contract/rent to own. It simply requires an extra month's down payment in advance."

She couldn't believe her luck. Could owning her own home be that easy? She didn't have much saved since having to pay rent on Sebastian's cottage, but with her current salary from Redmond's, she might be able to swing it by the end of the month. Now that she had a full-time job. If she were frugal.

"It might be doable. I'd like to take a couple of days to consider my finances and get back to you, if that's okay?"

"Yes. Of course. Here's my card." Jessica pulled a business card from her pocket and handed it to her. "Give me a call, and we can discuss the contract stipulations."

After saying their goodbyes, Nora drove Jackie home and then drove up to Grant's Lake. It was a seasonably warm day. A perfect day to walk around the man-made lake, clear her mind, and contemplate her next move. She hadn't been there since Sebastian's death, not wanting to have people look at her as if she were the scum of the earth. But this was part of letting go and moving on, as Jackie would say. It was time to start getting out, free her inner inhibitions, and start to enjoy life again.

Twenty minutes later, she parked the car and headed toward the sidewalk that meandered through a tree-lined walkway toward a sandy shoreline. From there she veered left and followed a trail into a nature-type area that led to a meadow, then back out next to the lake and a small dock jutting out into the water. Benches were strategically placed where one could sit and observe any wildlife, birds, and an occasional fisherman. She found an empty bench and settled in. Although the air was still a bit cool this time of year, it was invigorating. She tucked her hands in her jacket pocket, leaned back, and contemplated her next move.

Could she afford to buy a house on her present salary? Would she be able to pursue her dream of owning her own CPA business? She needed the job at Redmond's, and although she hadn't been there long, she knew it was a good fit and the money was more than adequate. If she pinched a few pennies, she could swing it. Getting out from under the burden of living in Sebastian's home was a necessity. Chuck's advances were getting more and more aggressive. If she had to wait a bit longer to set up her own business, she could handle it, financially. And the house she and Jackie had just looked at was perfect. She'd go home, take another look at her finances, check with the bank tomorrow, and hope things fell into place.

****

Two days later, she got a call from the realtor. The house was hers if she wanted to come in and sign the papers.

"You'll have to wait until the end of the month before you can move in," Jessica said. "I hope that works for you."

"Perfect. I'm double-checking with the bank Thursday morning to make sure I'm all set for a loan for the down payment. I'll stop by afterward."

"I'll see you then."

She stared out the office window, a broad smile on her face. It was really happening. She had to call Jackie. Tell her the fantastic news. But first she had to contact the bank and hope like hell she was going to be able to work something out in order to pull off obtaining the down payment.

She needed to ask Gavin for time off so she could go to the bank.

He was in his office when she returned from lunch, leaning over his desk. She tapped on his open door. He looked up, a frown on his face. He obviously wasn't happy about something. Perhaps it wasn't the time to ask.

"Is there a problem?" he asked as he closed the file he'd been studying.

"Not really. I'm in the process of buying a home and need to meet with the bank and my realtor on Thursday at ten thirty, and I need some time off. I'll be gone for a couple of hours. I wasn't sure if you wanted someone to cover the office while I was away from my desk or close until I return."

"I didn't realize you were looking for a house. Is everything okay? Do you need help with anything?"

"No. I'm fine, thanks. I've been wanting to find another place to live for some time. The opportunity finally presented itself."

"Are you sure this is the right move? Do you want me to help with any of the arrangements? Make sure everything is in order?"

It was exactly what she didn't want. She was going to do this on her own. She needed to do this on her own. It was a major part of her moving on, becoming her own woman.

"I have it under control. But thanks for the offer. It shouldn't take long."

"Of course you can have time off. Take whatever time you need. I'll be in the office all day Thursday. If I need help, I'll ring Bethany to sit the front office."

"Thank you."

"Thank you. You've been a real asset to the company. I appreciate all you've done for me. If you need anything, please don't hesitate to let me know."

"I appreciate the opportunity to work for you. You've already been more than generous." She felt as if they were running a mutual admiration society, and almost smiled.

"Good luck."

"Is there anything I can do for you this afternoon? You were looking a bit tense when I knocked."

"I was puzzling over the McClintock situation. If Coleman Baker calls, send it through to the lab. I'll be in there the rest of the day."

On her way back to her office, she stopped in the make-shift kitchen and prepared a steaming cup of coffee, the aroma of hazelnut trailing behind her as she returned to her desk. Things were looking up. She had a meeting with the bank at ten thirty on Thursday, and then was scheduled to meet with the realtor at eleven thirty. If everything worked out, she'd be back in the office by one o'clock, a new home owner.

Her insides warmed at the thought.

****

With Gavin out of the office the following two days, she established an office routine. She answered phone calls from several applicants wanting to apply for her position. There were several calls from a handful of Gavin's clients who either left messages or had his cell number and would call him directly. Emails from clients requesting appointments or canceling them due to conflicts were few, but she responded, arranged new appointments, and checked all the accounts.

Tuesday afternoon without warning, Gavin informed her she was to accompany him on board his boat while they conducted business out on Frenchman

Bay the following morning. It was time she got a sense of what he did while he was away from the office and out on his boat. Hopefully, it would give her a chance to become more in tune with his business and thus able to relate to his clients' needs.

"We'll leave first thing in the morning. Eric will have the boat waiting for us alongside the main dock. Bethany will cover the office while we're gone."

Wow. He had her organizational skills beat!

"And she's okay filling in at a moment's notice?"

"Of course. Like I said, it was a family business long before I took over. She knows enough about the business to handle whatever comes up. She's filled in before, so it won't be a problem."

Why wasn't she surprised? Beth's proprietorial actions while she'd visited the other day suddenly made sense. His sister's confidence was well earned.

"Is there anything in particular I need to know before we depart?"

"We'll be gone all morning, so wear something appropriate—and warm. You might want to bring sunscreen. Even this time of year, the sun out on the water can cause a burn. From the looks of your skin, I suspect you'd burn easily."

That wasn't the information she wanted, but for him to even consider her skin type and worry about it burning made her insides squirm. Was he this considerate of everyone? The look on his face and those devilishly sexy eyes gave nothing away. She steeled herself against the emotions bubbling inside. Being on a boat, in close proximity with Gavin Redmond, wasn't a good idea. But did she have a choice? She needed this job now, more than ever.

Although she knew who his clients were, their accounts, and his daily routine, she hadn't had time to become familiar with the major details of his clients' projects, or what he was involved in when he was sequestered in his lab or out on his boat. Including the McClintock case. He'd been rather discreet in that regard. Perhaps tomorrow's day at sea would be more enlightening as far as those accounts were concerned.

"Am I to assume you will be working on one of your projects while we're in Frenchman Bay?" she couldn't help asking. "Is it for the McClintock account?"

"Yes, as a matter of fact, it is. As you are aware, they are one of our main accounts. I assume that won't be a problem?"

"Of course not. Unless you've changed your mind and it is for you?"

"Never. I'll see you tomorrow morning at six a.m. on the docks."

****

Wednesday's unusually heavy early morning mist surrounded Nora as she walked past the closed storefronts toward the Bar Harbor pier. Coffee shops were open, however, and the nutty aroma mingled with the misty sea scents of seaweed and fish. Activity along the docks thrived as crews prepared their trawlers for a day of fishing on the Bay and farther out into the Atlantic. She couldn't resist the urge to purchase a large latte to go and sipped it as she searched for Gavin's boat. The hot, sweet liquid slid down her throat, soothing the anxiety and anticipation of spending a day out on the water with Gavin.

Business! Only business. Nothing personal about

the outing.

Sebastian had never taken her out on his boat. Or any boat, for that matter. Yet he had lived to be out on the water and had known what dangers could befall an errant seaman, which added to the mystery of why he had taken his boat out during a storm. He should have known better. Had he been that upset with her after their spat? Had she driven him to his death? Those thoughts had run through her mind a million times, nearly driving her crazy. But she knew better now. It hadn't been her fault. The guilt had lifted from her shoulders—finally.

Gavin was already on board when she approached the vessel, a no-frills, mid-sized fishing trawler. He met her on the dock and helped her aboard. "Right on time. We're about to set sail. Eric is waiting for us at the bow."

She clasped his outstretched hand and followed him toward the front of the ship. A man was bent over a large cooler. He resembled a pirate, with his muscular form and long, dark, curly hair tucked around ears and hidden underneath a sailor's cap. He straightened and smiled. His teeth winked out from under a full mustache.

"Nora, this is Eric, my assistant. You've talked to him on the phone."

"Hi, Eric. Good to finally meet you face to face."

"Well, I have to agree. Putting that pretty face to the lovely voice I hear on the phone has made my day. Where have you been hiding her, Gavin?"

Nora smiled, aware the young man was flirting with her, and was surprised at Gavin's quick reprimand.

"You know better, Eric. Are we all set to get this

crate underway?"

"I am, but you'll have to check with the skipper," Eric said. "Al's at the helm ready to get underway whenever you are."

"Behave yourself while I have a word with him." Gavin raised his eyebrows at his assistant, nodded, and then went to find the skipper, leaving her to fend for herself with Eric.

She spotted a wooden bench along the side railing and took advantage of it, putting space between her and Eric.

"So. You're Gavin's new hire? How much do you know about our operations so far?" Eric's playful demeanor turned serious.

She was relieved to not have the man come on to her for real. She didn't want to have to be rude and put him in his place if he made a pass toward her. "Not as much as I'd like," she said. "I hope to remedy that today."

"We've been monitoring the pollution in the area from a variety of land and marine uses," Eric explained. "We store the samples at ocean temperature in the coolers until Gavin gets them back to the lab."

"What form of pollution?"

"Good question. Substandard ships and poor shipping practices can cause considerable pollution. Which, as you can imagine, is not good for marine life and thus for the fishing industry. Gavin goes below and gathers water samples, as well as the sediment from the ocean floor, and then takes them back to his lab for evaluation."

Eric's nautical good looks as he made his way to untie the cords attached to the dock made her grin. A sexy pirate for sure with the confident sway of his hips and lopsided grin as he walked past her.

Five minutes later, the boat was under motion, and Gavin was by her side dressed in a wet suit. Lost for words, she couldn't help but stare at the virile man standing before her, his every muscle delineated in the tight, slick suit.

"Where are we headed?" she asked when she found her tongue.

"Toward Lobster Cove," Gavin said, pointing to the narrow bay to their right. "Coleman Baker thinks something or someone is tampering with his traps and fishing nets. Their nets are empty when they pull them in. We need to check the area. See if we can find anything that might help us figure out what's going on."

"We've been monitoring the waters," Eric added, joining them, arms crossed over his chest as he gazed out over the water. "A month ago, the harbormaster reported an incident of wastewater discharge by a small passenger vessel next to the town pier. We've been monitoring the waters. The Coast Guard is keeping an eye out for other occurrences, as well."

"How often does this happen?" she asked, the morning breeze blowing through her hair as the boat treaded water. "What about the bigger cruise ships? Do they pose a threat as well?"

She had seen the mid-size cruise ships in the harbor and often dreamed of sailing away to tropical locations on one of them. She hadn't considered they could be detrimental to fishermen and marine life, not only in Frenchman Bay, but around the world.

"Of course," Eric answered. "There have been incidences. But even with stricter laws over the past few years, it continues to happen."

"Doesn't the pollution affect other marine life close by? Or are the McClintock traps the only ones affected?"

"Although others have had lower catches, the McClintock's traps seem to be a major target in this area," Gavin said. "Others up along the Canadian coast have been having problems, too. I'm going to take samples of the ocean floor, as well as pull a few traps to take back to the lab and test. Do you scuba dive?"

"No. I didn't know it was a requirement for the job."

"It's not, but we'll have to remedy that," Gavin stated as he checked his gear.

"Not in this lifetime." She shook her head and stepped back as if he'd expected her to suit up right then and there. "Breathing underwater is not my strong point."

"We'll see." He dismissed her rejection of his suggestion. "In the meantime, make yourself comfortable and enjoy the ride. Help yourself to coffee below." Gavin pointed to the galley entrance. "And an extra blanket if you get cold. It can be a bit brisk out on the water this early in the morning. But when the clouds dissipate and the sun is overhead, it'll be hot. Hope you remembered your sunscreen."

"Yes." But she hadn't anticipated the cool morning air to turn so cold as the boat gained speed. A steady breeze grew stronger. Her hair flew about her face. She needed to tie it down, or she'd be fighting it all morning. But first, coffee. And then a blanket. Her lightweight jacket was not heavy enough to withstand the early morning chill out on the ocean.

When she returned on deck, coffee in hand, the boat slowed and then stopped. Gavin jumped onto the edge of the railing, ready to plunge backward into the frigid ocean. Eric stood by, ready to monitor his dive. She hadn't worked for Gavin very long, but she was already aware he didn't waste time. He didn't sit still, either. If he wasn't in his lab, he was meeting clients. More often than not, he was out on the water checking fishing regions and taking samples. He didn't depend on others. He might be abrupt with those he worked with, but she'd also come to recognize he wasn't being intentionally harsh. He had his mind on many projects and problems, and the pressure to find the answers, so he could move on to the next project, kept him going. He didn't suffer fools gladly, as her grandfather used to say.

Gavin leaned on the edge of the boat and dropped overboard, leaving a sharp ocean spray like ice splinters piercing her cheeks in its wake. She wiped at them as Gavin let the weight of the heavy tank submerge him into the deep, dark depths of the frigid water. She cringed at the thought of learning to dive. She gulped, took a full swallow of coffee, and let it slide down her throat and warm her insides. She drew closer to the railing, hugging the hot mug between her hands, and studied the spot where Gavin had disappeared.

"He's fine," Eric said, joining her. "He's done this a million times. He knows what he's doing."

"How long does he stay below?"

Eric chuckled. "Don't worry. He'll be quick. He's methodical, has it all worked out before he dives."

"It's got to be freezing down there."

"The wet suit is insulated against the cold. Like I

71

said, he'll be quick. If he finds anything unusual, he'll take samples of anything that looks suspicious. Even if something doesn't. He'll take pictures of traps and the entire area. He uses it to compare to other sights and pictures he's already taken. He'll use these to show his clients—see if they notice anything odd. Could be someone or some other business is poaching, causing the catch to be lower than usual. If it's environmental, he'll find out."

She'd heard Gavin talking on the phone to several clients this past week in regards to the possibility of other companies with ties to an Asian group with a higher than normal catch recently. However, he had kept that piece of information from her. Whether on purpose or because he had felt there was no need to inform her of all his business dealings, she assumed it was a case of her not needing to know.

"No pun intended, but Gav will get to the bottom of this one." Eric laughed as he prepared for Gavin's return on deck.

****

Ten minutes later, Gavin broke through the surface, threw his goggles over his head, and shook the water from his hair. He swam to the ladder hanging over the edge of the boat where Eric was waiting to retrieve the samples he had collected.

"Get them in the cooler," Gavin instructed. "Then tell Al to get under motion and head northeast up along the coast while I change into dry clothes and get a coffee."

He looked at Nora and smiled. Her crimson cheeks glowed, and her smooth complexion and shivering lips had urges running rampant through his veins. Strong emotions he hadn't felt in a long time. He didn't want to analyze why. He didn't need the distraction.

"You did leave me some coffee, didn't you?" he asked, as he sat on the bench to remove his flippers.

"A fresh pot's waiting."

He brushed past her and all but jumped into the galley to put distance between them. What was he thinking? He shouldn't have brought her. She was a distraction he could live without. Okay, so he'd thought she needed to know more about his company, his job. It had nothing to do with wanting to spend more time with her. Really. Still, he hadn't been able to get her out of his mind all the while he'd been down below. And, dammit, he'd almost missed seeing the knife wedged under the rock and sediment. If it hadn't been for the reflection off the silver blade from his light, he would have missed it.

Dammit! He had to focus on the job at hand, not Nora.

Dressed, warmed, and coffee mug in hand, he joined her and Eric up on deck.

"I was about to come looking for you."

Her smile made his temperature rise despite the cold breeze blowing over the bow and his damp hair.

"I needed a minute to change and collect my thoughts." He didn't mention what thoughts needed collecting. Thankfully, she didn't ask.

Nora had fulfilled the position beyond his expectations in only a week and a half. She was efficient, friendly to his clients, organized, and hadn't been put off by his blunt demeanor. She'd be an asset to any employer. He was lucky she'd appeared on his doorstep without meeting his sister first.

Eric's grin, however, was in need of being wiped off his know-it-all face.

"I didn't see anything untoward below," he told Eric as he sipped his coffee and diverted the conversation back to his clients' business. "Nothing. However, the traps were empty. I'll check the film from the hidden cameras when I get back to the lab, see if it shows anything."

He finished his coffee and kept to himself the fact he'd found and retrieved the knife. It looked as if one of the cameras had been tampered with, as well. He hoped it might still reveal a clue. Anything to help him make sense of what was going on.

"Let me know if you want me to do more surveillance farther north," Eric said. "In the meantime, I'll work with Al and keep an eye out for any odd-acting fishermen in this area."

"Good idea, thanks."

They were sailing close to the Canadian shoreline. The sun had risen, and the temperature had become milder. He joined Nora on the bench along the railing and looked out to sea.

"Are you warm enough since the sun finally decided to come out from under the heavy mist?"

"Actually, if it weren't for the cool breeze when the boat was in motion, I would have been fine. It's turning out to be a lovely day. Thanks for inviting me along. I don't often get out on the water. I'm enjoying seeing the coastline from this perspective. It's beautiful."

"I'm surprised. With the population of people living this close to the coast, I assumed most everyone took advantage of boating or watersports."

"Not always an option. Been a bit busy earning a living. It doesn't leave time to enjoy water sports of any kind, including fishing. An occasional outing like this is a treat. Again, thanks."

"We'll have to get you out more often, then. So what do you do for fun?"

"Not much, lately. I took care of my grandmother before she died. She raised me, so it was a pleasure to be by her side in her time of need. After I graduated from college, she became so ill I didn't have much time for fun."

Unlike him, who hadn't been there for his wife in her time of need because of his military career, Nora had given up her dream to care for her grandmother. The woman had a heart of gold.

"Then why are you working for me?"

"I need the capital. I've been working, trying to start up my own CPA business. And obtain a location to open my business. Thus the needed time off tomorrow in order to close on a house I've found."

"Congratulations. Good luck with the closing. Let me know if you need any help setting up your business. I have a few clients who could use your help. Me included."

"Thanks, but it'll be a while before I can actually get the business established. So you aren't getting rid of me so easily."

"Keep in mind I'd be happy to help."

He really didn't want to lose her as an employee, but she was efficient enough to run her own company, and he wasn't about to hold anyone back from their dreams.

"So what do you do for fun?" she asked, turning

the tables on him. "Seems like being out on the ocean is more work than fun."

"Actually, it's rather relaxing. But for fun, I enjoy working with children, especially children of veterans. Many of their fathers or mothers are deployed a lot, and they need the support. It's my way of continuing to support the troops and give back."

"I'm sure they all appreciate your service to home and country. Is that why you help coach soccer?"

"Exactly. I noticed you at the game the other night. Do you attend often?"

"On occasion. My friend Jackie's two boys play. They are the next best thing to a family of my own."

"You'll have to join us for the team's get-together at the end of the season, then."

"I'll think about it, thanks."

"Ah, I see Al has turned the boat around and is heading back to Bar Harbor. If you'll excuse me, I need to speak with Eric before we return to port. Stick around when we get back, and I'll take you to lunch. We don't have to go to Mariner's this time. There's a lobster shack on our way back to the office."

He quickly joined Eric, not giving her a chance to refuse.

Half an hour later, he and Eric secured the boat and gathered their equipment and cooler with the samples. He waited for Nora to join them and then helped her onto the dock.

"Give me about ten minutes, and you can follow me to the lobster pound. You won't be disappointed."

Chapter Six

Thursday morning, Nora's stomach rumbled in anticipation of meeting with the bank and then with Jessica Martin. True to Gavin's words, Bethany showed up to sit in for her while she was away from the office. Gavin had gone out on the boat earlier and wasn't going to be back, as planned, until late afternoon. Thankfully, his sister was pleasant, went directly to the kitchen for a coffee, and came back to the front office with a smile on her face.

"I hear you're in the process of purchasing a house today. Good luck. I hope everything goes smoothly."

"Thank you. I appreciate you filling in for a couple hours."

"Not a problem. Is there anything in particular I should be aware of before you leave?"

"Not unless Gavin has talked to you about something I might not be aware of. I'm sure you know how to get in touch with him."

"Yes. I think I can hold down the fort while you're gone."

She was surprised at Bethany's pleasant demeanor. She was sure Gavin's sister would have no problem handling anything that might come up while she was gone.

"I'll be back as soon as I can, hopefully by one o'clock." She tucked her purse strap over her shoulder and left the office and Bethany drinking her coffee.

Her meeting at the bank went without a hitch. By the time she finished with the realtor, she was on her way to being an actual homeowner. Papers were signed, and her first month's payment was transferred.

She quickly called Jackie with the news. "It's a done deal, Jackie. In fact, if I want to, I can move in right after Memorial Day. But I can take anything I want to the house as soon as I pick up the key."

"Exciting," Jackie squealed over the phone. "Let me know when you're ready to start packing, and I'll be there to help, girlfriend."

"Thanks. I'll give you a call. I'm going to get my car tires taken care of and then start packing Saturday morning."

"I'll bring the bubbly."

"Sounds like a plan. I'll see you then. I've got to get back to work. Gavin's sister is sitting the office, and I don't want to give her any reason to find fault with me, like being later than anticipated."

"His sister is filling in for you? Oh, my. Go. We'll chat later."

When she returned to the office, Bethany did a quick rundown on what had transpired while she was gone, congratulated her on becoming a home-owner, then didn't waste time excusing herself before leaving. As Gavin was out of the office the remainder of the day, Nora quickly caught up on everything before heading home.

The following day, Gavin was once again out on the boat with Eric. She was about to leave work late afternoon when the phone rang.

"Redmond's Marine Resources Management, Ms.

Spears speaking."

"Hi, Nora. This is Bethany. Is Gavin in?"

"No, he's out on the boat with Eric again today."

"Darn it. I forgot to remind him he needs to be at the cemetery, in uniform, for the Memorial Day services and honors Monday morning at ten o'clock sharp. It'd be just like him to forget."

Nora had already discerned Gavin wasn't the type to forget anything, especially something as important as attending a Memorial Day service if he was required to be there.

"I can leave him a message, but you might want to try his cell phone."

"Tried that. He's probably too far out on his boat or underwater. I'll give him a call later. Will I see you at the festivities?"

"I'm not sure I can make it to the cemetery, but I planned to be at the park."

If it weren't for joining Jackie to watch her boys march with the Cub Scouts, she had planned to skip this year's event. It might have been more than a year, but she didn't relish the idea of receiving stares from the community's higher echelons after her spectacular spectacle at Sebastian's burial. And she wasn't anxious to return to the scene of her outburst while people who had witnessed her pathetic display were there visiting their loved ones. Sitting quietly on the sidelines at the soccer games wasn't as obvious as showing her face at one of Lobster Cove's major events.

****

Nora drove her car to the cemetery next to St. Joseph's Church Saturday after having her tires replaced. American flags flew at every lamp post around Lobster Cove's central square, along Maple Avenue, Main Street, Oak Avenue, and First Street, in preparation for Monday's Memorial Day celebration. Both docks across from the square had been outfitted with flags on either side of the boardwalk, and many of the local boats and the majority of the trawlers flew their flags with pride. Memorial Day specials were offered at the various restaurants, bakeries, bars, and other niche shops for the weekend. The new owners of Flowers in Bloom were doing a bang-up business with their annuals, as well as urns lining the sidewalk outside their store, filled with blood-red geraniums and powdery mint dusty millers.

She drove her car into St. Joe's empty parking lot and parked along the back, under a large oak tree. She shut the motor off, pressed her lips together, and shut her eyes. Could she do it? Could she get out of the car and visit Sebastian's gravesite? She hadn't been back to the cemetery since that notable day when she'd made a complete ass of herself. Hadn't been able to get past the anguish, the fear, and the stupidity of her actions. But it was time. Time to say her goodbyes and move on.

Scanning the area, she checked to make sure no one was around to witness her final farewell to Sebastian. She opened the car door, stepped out, stood for a moment, and panned the area. Relieved no one was on hand to see her make a fool of herself once again over Sebastian, she locked the door and walked, as if in a trance, toward the open cemetery gates. She took a deep breath and entered. Heavy scents of pine and damp earth filled the air. The coolness surrounding the tree-lined avenue and in between the headstones sent chills along her spine. Her insides quivered. She mentally shook herself, lifted her head, pulled her shoulders back, and moved forward, step by step, until she stood in front of Sebastian's gravesite. Flowers adorned the immediate area. A large urn to the left was filled to overflowing with geraniums. Tall spikes spilled out from the center of the pot, and an assortment of wave petunias and dusty millers were snuggled in around the edges. It resembled the arrangements she'd seen on the sidewalk outside Flowers in Bloom.

She walked up to the front of the headstone, silently read the inscription, and felt...nothing. Nothing! No heartache. No twinges of hope for what might have been. Nothing but sadness over the loss of a life. She turned, spotted a wooden bench on the far side of the path, and hanging her head, wandered over and sat.

After all the tears she'd shed at Sebastian's funeral, the days and nights of longing for his touch again, his kisses, his presence, she didn't have a tear left in her. She thought about the hurt, the humiliation, the betrayal when she'd discovered he'd never planned to divorce Juelle. It had eased her shame when she'd discovered he'd been seeing someone else, cheating on both her and Juelle. The man had been a first-class jerk, a player. He had never really loved her. How had she even thought she loved him? And, good Lord, what kind of person did that make her?

Pathetic.

Never again! She vowed to never again let another man get to her the way Sebastian had used her. Her guard was firmly in place. She'd learned her lesson the hard way. It would be a cold day in hell before she'd let any man use her again.

Now, sitting alone in the shaded silence, she recalled her actions the day they buried Sebastian. Surrounded by her friends, she'd sobbed hysterically, bent over in anguish. She'd broken free from the group and flew at Juelle, her arms waving like a madwoman, screaming at Sebastian's wife. "You killed him," she had shrilled like a banshee. She'd even called Juelle a bitch and told her she didn't deserve him. But being distraught at losing Sebastian, she'd even gone so far as to tell Juelle she deserved to die for what she'd done to Sebastian. At the time, she'd believed Juelle had told the doctors to remove Sebastian's life support. Did Juelle have any inkling he had been going to seek a divorce? If Juelle hadn't pulled the plug on him, she knew he would have followed through with the divorce and married her. However, looking back, she didn't realize then that he'd been cheating on her as well as Juelle. She had fallen to the ground on bended knees, gulping for air between sobs, her friends by her side. Reliving the moment made her regret her actions that day.

Silence surrounded the snug alcove planked by budding hydrangea bushes not yet in bloom. The well-tended hillside cemetery contained many such secluded mourning areas where one could rest, reflect on their loved one's passing, and celebrate their life. But her reflections were not so angelic or honorable. No. Her reflections centered on why she needed to visit Sebastian's grave after all this time. The answer? She needed closure.

What had she seen in him? What had drawn her to him? Yes, he'd been a charismatic man and handsome. They had met at a July Fourth celebration. She hadn't known about his wife—he hadn't worn a ring. She'd been walking along the pier, tripped on one of the loose boards, and almost fell into the bay when he caught her and pulled her into his strong arms. He'd invited her for coffee at one of the cafés along the pier. She'd willingly agreed. The rest was history. He'd been charming, witty, and attentive. She'd recently broken off her relationship with Dustin, thanks to his infidelity. On top of that, her grandmother had fallen and broken her hip. After a long rehabilitation, she had died of pneumonia. Her grandmother had raised her after her parents' deaths when she was ten, and she had no one to turn to at the time. Yearning for love and affection, she'd soaked up Sebastian's warmth and caring like a woman dying of thirst on a parched desert. What bothered her the most was her asinine behavior at his burial, in front of the entire town of Lobster Cove as her witnesses.

Tears escaped, slid between her cold fingers. She wiped her face with trembling hands. Good Lord, she'd made a bigger mess of her life than she'd bargained for—there was no end to her shame.

****

Gavin knelt next to his wife's headstone, closed his eyes, and sighed. He missed her. Had Celina already been gone two years? It seemed like forever. She had gone through so much the two years before her death, especially once the cancer took hold, filling her body. And although his wife no longer suffered, it didn't ease his guilt at not having been there for her when she needed him the most. He'd let his own priorities take precedence before he'd realized how sick she had been. She had kept her sickness to herself.

How the hell did his sister expect him to even think

about another relationship, let alone a temporary fling, so soon? Just because his mother had moved on and remarried after his father's death didn't make it any easier for him to do the same. His father had been in a VA home for so long his mother had lived on her own for years.

He laid his hand on the top of the etched headstone. It was cold to the touch. He removed his hand, stood back, placed a single rose at the bottom of the cement pad, and shook his head. He looked out over the wide expanse of the rows and rows of headstones and monuments. Several had small flags next to them, identifying them as veterans, reminding him he had to attend the annual memorial services on Monday. His mother expected it. Truth be told, he expected it of himself. Not so much for him, but for the others. He needed to honor those who gave so much for their country. He knew the price many had paid, including his father.

He closed his eyes and whispered an "I miss you" to his wife, and then, hands in his pants pockets, wound his way along a narrow path to the left, toward his father's plot. And spotted Nora Spears sitting on a bench. Her head was bowed, her hands clasped tightly in her lap. For a moment, he had the strongest urge to go to her, comfort her. The slight breeze and silence drifting through the cemetery washed over him. He had wanted to come and visit Celina's resting place without family or a crowd of onlookers before Monday morning. He didn't need anyone witnessing his grief. He assumed Nora Spears was of the same mind. He didn't want to encroach on her private visit with Sebastian McClintock.

About to turn away, he took another moment to observe her in her time of sorrow. Nora raised her head and spotted him. His heart ached at the raw emotions etched on her tearstained face. He knew her grief. Losing a loved one had taken the zest for life right out of him. Unable to turn and leave without offering condolences, he slowly made his way to her side. The old wooden bench creaked as his body settled in, and he rested against the back.

"I assume you've decided, as I have, to come for a visit before the crowds descend Monday morning?"

She wiped her tearstained face with the back of her hand and sucked in a deep breath, letting it out slowly between trembling lips. "Yes. It would be difficult to stalk your lover's gravesite while their family was nearby."

"Nora, I wasn't insinuating anything."

"That's okay. I know Bethany has more than likely filled you in, unless you were already up to date on all the old gossip."

"Lobster Cove is a small community, and having the McClintocks as one of my clients, I'm bound to hear things. Doesn't mean I have to believe everything I hear."

"You should. They're more than likely all true. Chalk it up to being green behind the ears, but I've certainly learned my lesson."

"Life is full of lessons. We all learn from our mistakes. Sometimes they're nothing more than not prioritizing what's really important in life before it's too late. It seems as if we both had to experience a loved one's death to appreciate what they truly meant to us."

"I know you're trying to comfort me, but in my case, I've learned the man I loved wasn't really in love with me, and I found out too late. Talk about a shock. My tears aren't for a lost love so much as for a lost life. Not to mention feeling sorry for myself over what a fool I made of myself in front of the entire town. So yes, I've no doubt the stories you've heard about me are true. I'm here today to pay proper respect. Nothing more."

"Very commendable of you."

"You're being too kind. I'm pretty sure you're the only one outside my circle of friends to think so. But thanks."

"Don't be too hard on yourself."

He patted her clasped hands. They were cold to the touch from the cool morning air. Concerned for the sadness in her eyes, he had the strongest urge to take her in his arms and comfort her.

"What about you?" Nora asked, shifting to the side. "I take it you were visiting your wife's resting place?"

"Yes, well, as much as I loved her, I had no idea what she was going through in the beginning. How she suffered." He sat back, his hands secure, once again, in his coat pockets. "When it finally hit me how ill she had become, it was too late. The cancer had progressed beyond hope."

"I'm sorry for your loss."

He'd heard those words so many times over the last year it didn't faze him any longer. They were nothing but words. Words hadn't consoled him then or made the hurt any less. How his sister thought he could walk away was beyond him. You didn't stop loving someone because they had died.

The sun shifted behind the trees, causing a shadow to fall over the stillness surrounding them. A squirrel scampered along the bushes across the way. Two birds twittered, flew overhead, and settled in a pine tree to the left.

Calmness settled inside his gut. He drew in a deep steadying breath and then rose. Nora also stood and gathered her blue peacoat collar tight around her neck. Her eyes found his. The misery he saw in them increased the urge to cradle her in his arms and hold her tight, soothe her frayed emotions. Instead, he clasped her shoulder in acknowledgement of a shared pain and then stepped back.

"If you'll excuse me, I want to visit my father's site while I'm here."

"I was about to leave, as well."

She looked embarrassed. He hadn't meant to upset her. He nodded and then turned down the path to his right, leaving her standing alone to face her own demons. He had plenty demons of his own needing attention.

Chapter Seven

Memorial Day arrived with the sun shining over Lobster Cove and the excitement of the day's events weighing on her mind. The May temperature along the coast was seasonally cool. She was glad she'd gone to the cemetery Saturday instead of waiting to visit Sebastian's gravesite today, not wanting to run across any of the McClintocks or their friends. She stayed outside the cemetery gates and kept to the side behind an old, gnarly, leafless maple tree where she could observe the proceedings in private.

The American Legion Color Guard stood at attention inside the cemetery entrance, waiting for the community organizations and general public to arrive. The American flag flew at half-mast. Exactly on the stroke of ten, the town supervisor stepped forward and announced the program to begin. Father Zack appeared and offered the opening prayer, and then a Legion member took his place at the podium and recited the World War I war poem "In Flanders Fields" by Lt. Colonel John McCrae:

> *In Flanders fields the poppies blow*
> *Between the crosses, row on row,*
> *That mark our place; and in the sky*
> *The larks, still bravely singing, fly*
> *Scarce heard amid the guns below.*
> *We are the Dead. Short days ago*

We lived, felt dawn, saw sunset glow,
Loved and were loved, and now we lie,
In Flanders fields.

A hush fell over the crowd, giving pause to reflect on the meaning of the words, which were then followed by the Legion's Women's Auxiliary singing "God Bless America." Within seconds, those who had gathered at the cemetery joined in, filling the hill high above Lobster Cove with patriotic sentiment. Immediately following, the seven color guards issued their twenty-one-gun salute, followed by a lone bugler from the high school band playing "Taps." Final statements were issued, and then Police Chief Daryl Johnson jumped in his squad car to initiate and lead the parade procession back to the town square.

The Legion Color Guard led those legionnaires who were able to march, followed by the Women's Auxiliary, the local Coast Guard, the Boy Scouts, and the Girl Scouts, to the beat of the high school drum corps and marching band's patriotic music. Bright orange poppies were worn by many, as well as being given out on the streets to those who didn't yet have one. Once the procession stepped out onto First Street, they turned down Maple Avenue where kids on their bicycles, horses and riders, and a few stragglers wanting to be included, joined the parade. The local ambulance and a few fire trucks brought up the rear.

Nora joined Jackie and the others as they walked along the sidewalks, following the parade through town to the main square next to the bay. Jackie's husband, Brad, was one of the color guards, while her boys, Timmy and Cody, marched with the Cub Scouts.

The parade turned down Main Street where flags

flew from many of the homes' front porches. The procession turned left, directly into the Town Park. Sea mist scents mingled with the odors coming from the grills filled with barbequed chicken, hot dogs, and hamburgers, as the morning sun rose and warmed the day. The parade marched toward the large white gazebo decorated in red, white, and blue bunting. Large wreaths adorned either side of the entrance as well as behind the podium in the center of the staging area. Small flags lined the perimeter of the gazebo, along with colorful potted plants. The band marched to the left, stopped, turned to those already assembled, and immediately started playing "America, The Beautiful" as others continued to fill the town square, waiting for the ceremonies to begin.

Nora was happy to observe from behind those wanting a front row view. Jackie had other ideas, however, and took her by the arm and tugged her through the crowd toward the front.

"Brad is one of those being honored today. I want to capture the moment with my camera."

"I'll wait here. You go ahead."

Nora dug in her heels and insisted they at least find a spot to the side where she wouldn't be up front and center. If it hadn't been for Jackie insisting she come to watch her boys in the parade and Brad receive an award, she wouldn't have come at all.

When she viewed those assembled in the gazebo, she was positive she shouldn't have come. Sebastian's mother, Eugenia McClintock, stood front and center, groomed to the nines from her salon-styled hairdo to her shiny, patent-leather, two-inch heels. Her red, white, and blue dress suit gave her a patriotic appearance to fit the occasion. Mark Logan was also there, standing tall in his uniform befitting a local war hero who had come back to Lobster Cove and now worked for Homeland Security. Juelle McClintock's best friend, Katelyn, Mark's wife, was sure to be close by. Another reason Nora preferred to remain hidden in the crowd. Dining at Mariner's Fish Fry with Gavin a couple weeks ago hadn't been easy, as it was Katelyn's family's diner. Though she'd managed. But bumping into Katelyn, face to face here at the park, was a different kettle of fish, something she didn't want to do.

The day was turning out to be a disaster.

Jackie waved to Brad, who was standing in the front row on stage along with other legionnaires. Gavin hadn't marched in the procession but stood in the background, a stern look on his face, an indication he was uncomfortable in his Air Force blues. Although not a shy man, he was an unassuming and humble man who didn't knowingly seek attention. He looked so eye-catching standing there her heart skipped a beat.

He spotted her, nodded. The smile he gave her made his dimples more pronounced. Their gazes locked, and her insides warmed to molten lava thinking about their encounter at the cemetery on Saturday afternoon. She averted her gaze, and dismayed, was met with Eugenia McClintock's infectious smile directed right at her, neatly breaking the spell between her and Gavin. She had a hard time reciprocating the woman's smile. But not wanting to be rude, she nodded in acknowledgment. If she could, she would have inched her way to the back of the crowd and right on out of the park. Instead, she tried her best to return the smile and was surprised when Mrs. McClintock nodded in return.

Thankfully, the American Legion commander, in full regalia, took the podium and welcomed everyone to "this auspicious occasion." All eyes were focused on him.

"We have four members who have earned high honors for their distinguished service and continuous work with our disabled veterans and fund-raising efforts here in Lobster Cove since their return from serving our beloved country," the commander addressed the crowd.

Brad, Gavin, Mark Logan, and Ernie Davis were called forward and each given a certificate of appreciation. The crowd erupted with cheers and thunderous applause while the band belted out another patriotic number. Once things quieted down, the commander called Eugenia McClintock forward.

"Many of you know Eugenia McClintock is an Auxiliary member of our great organization and has graciously donated funds in her son Sebastian's name to the local veteran's hospital. It is with deep appreciation that we recognize her for this wonderful donation. This gift will go a long way to help our wounded vets and their families."

Eugenia didn't hesitate to step forward, clear her throat, and scan the park with a bright smile on her face that about outdid the sun. Not one to shy away from the public eye, Eugenia presented a confidant air and an assumed gratitude as she accepted the award without hesitation.

As anticipated, the crowd cheered and clapped.

"Thank you everyone." Eugena stepped to the microphone and scanned the crowd. "As you know, although I no longer am a shareholder of the

McClintock's, I still have the privilege to allocate funds from endowments for local causes. However, this particular asset became available, thanks in part to one of our citizens, and is earmarked for the rehabilitation of our local wounded vets. Therefore, I wish to acknowledge Nora Spears for her considerate and selfless donation to this worthy cause. Thank you, Ms. Spears."

The stunned silence rang in Nora's ears. She hadn't expected Eugenia McClintock to be so vocal in regards to her gift. Actually, her refusal to take Sebastian's money couldn't be considered a gift. Eugenia had been extremely vocal in the beginning about who the money belonged to. It didn't matter. She hadn't wanted any part of it. But Mr. Jordan had explained the details of the will, and so she'd decided to donate the money to the McClintock fund for wounded vets. At least it would be put to good use. Why Eugenia had embarrassed her by formally announcing to the world that she had donated the money as a gift, she had no idea. It wasn't as if she had a ton of money to give away. She wanted the ground to open and swallow her. But then someone—Gavin—started clapping, and others followed suit.

Oh, God. All eyes were on her.

She met Gavin's eyes and his warm appreciative smile. Her head grew light, her knees weak. Jackie wrapped her arm around her shoulders as the crowd clapped, filling the square with their appreciation.

"Buck up, girlfriend. Eugenia McClintock has welcomed you back into the community with open arms in front of the entire town."

"I'm not sure it's where I want to be."

"Smile. Let them know you're not hiding your head in the sand any longer."

She smiled, mouthed a thank you to Eugenia McClintock, and was shocked when Jackie turned her around to face the crowd. What she didn't see on everyone's faces was condemnation, anger, or even pity. Relieved, she smiled, nodded, and sighed. She leaned into Jackie before her knees gave out.

The band erupted into another marching song after the commander's farewell address.

"Can we go now? I need to assimilate all this."

"I'd love to go with you, but I have to collect my boys. Brad and I are taking them on a whale-watching tour this afternoon. Robert Matheson and his niece Sandra Godfrey are offering a special tour for the scouts and their families this afternoon."

"OMG, Jackie, you can't leave me." She followed Jackie as her friend headed toward the scouts. "Why would she do such a thing? Why would Eugenia McClintock put me on the spot in front of the entire town? We hadn't exactly parted in good terms when I refused the money from the bank."

"Maybe she's trying to atone for her son's less-than-perfect actions. Since her husband and son died, she and Mr. Jordan have become an item. Maybe she's learned a thing or two about being humble this past year. Or discovered her son wasn't such a nice boy after all. I know everyone thinks highly of Mr. Jordan."

"You could be right."

"Not to change the subject, but I believe your new employer is headed this way."

Along with an older couple, Gavin and his sister Bethany were making their way in her direction.

"Gotta go get the boys. Good luck. Call me later. Better yet, stop over for a barbeque this evening. Brad's ribs are to die for." Jackie waved her hand over her shoulder as she disappeared through the throng milling around the gazebo. She puzzled at her friend's quick exit.

Bethany was the first to speak.

"Congratulations, Nora. A huge kudo from Eugenia McClintock goes a long way in Lobster Cove. Her nod is sure to boost Gavin's connection with them."

"I can assure you, it wasn't my intent. It has nothing to do with your brother's company. That money was earmarked over a year ago."

"Nevertheless," Gavin interjected, "it was an honorable thing to do. Thank you. I see we have a mutual interest. Your donation will go a long way to help our local vets and their families."

He extended his hand, and she complied as his hand swallowed hers. The hold, firm and warm, unnerved her and had the strangest sensations coursing through her insides to the point she had difficulty breathing. He continued to hold her hand as he returned her gaze. She steeled herself not to show how much his touch affected her equilibrium, and how it knocked her off-kilter.

"I should be congratulating you, as well," she said. "Thank you. And thank you for your service."

"My pleasure." He released her hand and stepped to the side. "May I introduce my mother and her husband, Jonathan and Sylvia Norton. And of course, you know Beth."

"It's so nice to finally meet you, my dear," Mrs.

Norton said, extending her hand. "I've heard a lot about you from both Beth and Gavin. Seems you're quite capable of dealing with both of my headstrong and outspoken children. It's rather refreshing."

It wasn't hard to imagine what Bethany had shared with her mother after the conversation they'd exchanged the first day they'd met. On the other hand, she had no idea what Gavin would have told his mother.

"It's nice to meet you both." Nora shook hands with Sylvia and Jonathan and let the matter drop. Gavin's family, Bethany aside, appeared to be friendly enough.

"I see your friend deserted you. Why not join us for lunch?" Gavin invited. "We're heading over to the Love Caters All truck next to the library." His look challenged her to accept.

"Why, what a lovely idea, Gavin," his mother encouraged. "Of course she'll join us."

"Mother, Nora might have other plans," Bethany chimed in. "Don't push."

Not missing Bethany's knowing smile, she found herself agreeing to join them.

"I'd love to join you for lunch. Thank you for inviting me." Since Jackie had deserted her, it was better than eating alone.

"No need to thank us. You deserve a treat as much as my son does. So instead of fighting off the crowd here, I suggest we go to Mariner's Fish Fry and sit out back on the deck overlooking the bay," Sylvia suggested. "It's such a lovely day. It will be much more relaxing, don't you think?"

She caught Gavin's raised eyebrows as if asking if

eating at Mariner's was going to be a problem. At this point, having already eaten there with him two weeks ago, and Eugenia's bombshell minutes ago, she was confident she could handle it. That was, unless Katelyn and Mark Logan showed up. But dealing with Gavin's entire family all at once was a daunting proposition on its own. Bethany's less-than-enthusiastic demeanor didn't help. But the challenging gleam in Gavin's eyes proved her undoing.

"I'd like that. Thank you," she heard herself say, aware Bethany's smile was less than heartfelt. Her stomach lurched. She hoped like hell she could handle it.

"Great. You can ride with Gavin. We'll meet you there," Sylvia said, taking her husband's arm, ready to leave.

"Not necessary. My car is parked next to the library. No need to backtrack to the park afterward."

"Suit yourself. Gavin, would you like to ride with us?"

"Thanks, Mom, but I'll drive my own car, as well. Give us a few minutes, and we'll join you shortly."

"We'll claim a table on the deck and wait for you there. Don't be too long. We had a light breakfast."

Jonathan hooked his hand on his wife's arm and led her around the gazebo, through the crowded grounds, and out of the park. Nora didn't miss the sly smirk on Bethany's face, as Gavin's sister hung back for several, long, drawn-out seconds before turning and following her mother.

"I hope you're not about to let Beth's behavior change your mind. You're perfectly safe."

"I didn't know I had anything to worry about in

regards to Bethany. I can assure you, she has nothing to worry about in regards to me."

"She's overly protective."

"Hard to believe, seeing as she's trying to set you up with anyone who comes along in a skirt."

"Not anyone. Why do you think she'd been vetting my hired help? She doesn't want me to fall into the wrong hands."

"Then she doesn't have to be concerned about me. As you and I discussed the other day, lessons learned."

"Exactly. So why don't you relax and enjoy the afternoon with us? My mother isn't one to pry into other people's business. She'll keep Beth in check."

"I'm not convinced anyone can keep Beth in check. Despite her strong personality, I do like her. She is open and forthcoming. At least one knows where they stand with her."

"Are you sure you don't want to ride with me?"

"Thanks, but I do want to stop for gas at Jay's before I go home later. It's on the way. I won't be long."

Gavin smiled. "Your organizational skills are one of the things I like about you, Nora. I'll wait for you in front of Mariner's."

He leaned over, and without warning, kissed her cheek. For what seemed like long seconds, he stared into her eyes, a smile on his face, before slipping his sunglasses in place and turning to make his way through the crowd and out of the town square.

A slight chill swam through her, a chill that had nothing to do with the breeze coming off Frenchman Bay. She reflected on their encounter in the cemetery the other afternoon when he'd covered her cold hands with his warm ones. He hadn't been his domineering self then. He'd been compassionate, caring. She had wanted to reach out to him and hold him then. She had wanted him to hold her. After his brief kiss on her cheek, she was beginning to long for something she knew wasn't a good idea. For sure, it wasn't a good idea to see him outside of the workplace. People would get the wrong impression. Family or no family, she refused to get entangled romantically with Gavin Redmond.

She made her way to the library parking lot next to Love Caters All's mobile van. Maya Cruz's grill master, Mickey Ruggiero, was already busy grilling meat. Mixed with the mouth-watering aroma of onions, peppers, and French fries, the odors swirled around the park, making her stomach rumble. Unlike Gavin's mother, she had skipped breakfast. She unlocked her car, slipped inside, pressed the ignition, and sat staring straight ahead in a trance. No. She refused to grow too fond of Gavin Redmond or his family. If she was smart, she'd drive straight home and bypass Mariner's. She'd look for another job and skip town altogether. There was nothing holding her here in Lobster Cove.

Nothing at all.

Well, except for the house she had just bought.

Chapter Eight

Startled by a knock on her car window, Nora snapped her head around to find Jackie's smiling face pressed against the pane. She lowered the window, raised her brow in question, and looked at her friend's inquisitive face.

"So you met the family?" Jackie's grin grew wider.

"Jackie? What the hell are you doing here? Weren't you going out on a whale-watching adventure with the kids?"

"We stopped to buy a picnic lunch to take with us. We were heading to the car when I saw you get in yours. So tell me, girlfriend. What's up?"

"What do you mean what's up? Nothing. Nothing at all."

"Really? The way I saw it, something was going on. A kiss?"

"How could you see from way over here? You're digging for morsels where there are none."

"Okay, but from your reaction to his kiss and that dreamy look on your face as you sit here contemplating heaven only knows what, I'm assuming you weren't immune to his advances."

"I'm having lunch with them at Mariner's as soon as you get out of my face so I can get underway. The kiss meant nothing, I can assure you. If you must know, it was a simple thank you. Gavin also donates to the local wounded vets program."

"Lunch with the family? A mutual interest? Oh, snap! I knew something was going on between you two. Enjoy your lunch with the parents."

"Jackie. Stop. Right. There. Nothing is going on. It was a kind offer to help celebrate our common interest in the wounded vets program. Nothing more."

"Okay, okay. I'll step aside. But we will talk later. Dinner at my place. Tonight. Don't be late. I want details."

Jackie reached in, wrapped her arms around her neck, kissed her cheek, and disappeared around the rear of the car. Nora sucked in a deep breath, let it whoosh out, and then backed the car out of the parking lot. And smiled. Jackie was a great friend. A bit wacky at times, but a great friend. Without a doubt she'd be on the phone later tonight wanting to know all about her luncheon with Gavin and his family if she didn't show up for Brad's famous barbeque.

Fortunately, there would be nothing to tell.

****

As promised, Gavin was waiting for her next to the entrance of Mariner's Fish Fry. She'd always been a sucker for a man in uniform, and Gavin Redmond was a sharp, prime example of "be all you can be" as he leaned against the building, hat in hand. The sun shone overhead in a cloudless sky, highlighting his sexy good looks. She wished she could see his eyes hiding behind those sunglasses, so she could determine what he was thinking. Sitting on the back deck would be a welcome relief, hopefully it would turn out to be a less stressful informal setting with his family.

Hopefully.

"I thought you might change your mind and not show." Gavin removed his sunglasses and raised his brows in question.

"How perceptive. However, your mother seemed sincere in her invitation. I didn't want to hurt her feelings."

"My mother's made of sterner stuff. She doesn't get upset over people turning her invitations down. Although I must admit, I'm glad you decided to show. I get the notion you don't get out much these days, and instead keep yourself hidden from the community. I hope Eugenia McClintock's recognition of your generous donation put a dent in your armor."

"It did take me by surprise. Although I wish she hadn't done it in front of the entire community." Gavin had no idea the money hadn't been hers to begin with, or the circumstances behind her giving it away.

He opened the door, ushered her past the reception area, through the busy restaurant, and in between fully occupied tables of happy diners, their plates piled high with fresh seafood. The smell of the ocean, along with the savory aroma of boiled clams, lobster, and buttered corn on the cob swirling around the diner as they made their way to the back deck entrance, teased her nose as they passed table after table filled with baskets of shrimp and lobster bowls.

As they approached the open doors leading to the deck, Gavin placed his hand on her shoulder, turned her toward him, and stared into her eyes. Several heartbeats later, he smiled, his eyes seeming to seek an answer from an unknown question. Her pulse raced in anticipation. He opened his mouth to speak, but Bethany stepped through the entrance.

"There you are. Mom was about to have Ed send out an APB on you two. He was able to call in off-duty and join us for lunch."

"Edward is Bethany's husband, by the way," Gavin informed her. "Glad he could make it, sis."

With that, Gavin ushered her out onto the deck, leaving her to wonder what he'd been about to say.

Sylvia stood as they stepped on the back deck. She waved them over to their table.

"Jon has already ordered a fried shrimp basket and champagne to celebrate. Come join us."

Gavin introduced Bethany's husband, Edward, a local cop, in uniform, tall, lanky, short dark hair, and handsome features with an engaging smile. He and Bethany made an adorable couple. Despite Bethany's usual hardnosed demeanor, she acted like a schoolgirl with a crush on the captain of the football team and didn't leave her husband's side during the entire meal. It gave Nora an entirely different perspective of Gavin's sister. Not having been intimidated by Bethany to begin with, she witnessed a caring side to Bethany she was sure most people probably didn't see. It was obvious why Bethany was searching for someone special for her brother. She wanted Gavin to have the same kind of love and happiness she had.

Bethany had nothing to fear from her in regards to Gavin. Gavin might be handsome as sin, but she wasn't about to get entangled in a relationship with her boss. Besides, she could tell from their talk at the cemetery he was still in love with his wife. She'd had enough of being second best, even if it was competing with a deceased spouse. Yet she wondered what the look was Gavin had given her right before Bethany had interrupted them. What had he been about to say?

The picnic tables on the back deck were situated so everyone had a bird's eye view of the bay. The harbor activity added to the colorful surroundings—a couple of speed boats kicked up waves, and in the distance, a tall sailboat and a cruise ship the size of an eleven-story building covering at least three city blocks were anchored for the day.

Gavin pulled a chair out for her and waited while she sat before he settled in next to her. Bethany and Edward sat on his left, and Sylvia and Jonathan on her right. She felt surrounded but warmed by the happy family atmosphere. She folded her hands in her lap and pasted a smile on her face. Other than Jackie's family, and not counting caring for her grandmother over the years, she hadn't been included in a family gathering like this in a long time.

"So a toast," Jonathan said as he poured the bubbly. He lifted his champagne flute, the sun sparkling off the liquid. "To our honorees and all the unsung heroes."

She lifted her glass along with the others and then sipped. The carbonated liquid burst into her mouth and caught her by surprise. She set the flute back on the table, gulped, and quietly tried to clear her throat. She didn't drink champagne as a rule, so the first sip of the carbonated bubbly was always an eye-opener when she did. Thankfully, the waitress came to take their orders so the others were distracted and didn't notice her minor dilemma. Or so she thought. Gavin reached behind and gently patted her back between her shoulder blades. His touch unnerved her, his kindness unexpected. Her skin tingled.

"Thank you. I'm fine." Drinking on an empty stomach could be embarrassing. The last thing she wanted to be in front of her employer, and his family, was an inebriated guest. She took a tiny sip of her celebratory drink, making sure not to overindulge until their meal arrived.

For the life of her, she didn't know what entrée she ordered, but the waitress left, and the conversation caught her attention.

"Did you know Gavin was wounded while serving in the military?" Bethany said and then sipped her champagne, looking over the rim, obviously waiting for Nora's stunned reaction.

"Beth. It's not important," Gavin chided. "A minor incident, nothing more. Hardly life threatening."

"But you did receive a Purple Heart. And you were a hero, saving all those men's lives."

"Just doing my job. Let it go."

"Still, Gavin," his mother interjected, "you are a hero and were honored for your heroic service. You should be recognized for the work you do with wounded vets and their families here at home."

"There are many others who earned the name hero and lost their lives. A bit of shrapnel in the leg is nothing to brag about. Ed knows what I'm talking about. In his line of work, he's seen the same."

"Like you, Gavin, it's all in the line of work," Ed chimed in, lifting his glass in toast again before taking another hearty sip.

She had no idea Gavin had suffered a leg injury, not to mention having received a Purple Heart. He certainly carried himself as if he hadn't sustained a leg wound. Wow! A Purple Heart. Her opinion of him ratcheted up a notch. She never would have suspected it of him. He might be forthcoming and confident and a bit overbearing at times, but then she could see him persevering in battle and saving others. A caring side hidden deep inside she'd recently had the opportunity to witness first hand. He was an honorable and compassionate man and helped coach a bunch of rowdy boys' soccer team, too.

"So, Gavin, how did your meeting with Coleman Baker go?" Jonathan asked, breaking into the tense conversation and her lingering thoughts. "Have you found any leads in the case?"

"He thinks it might have something to do with a string of nets being harvested before they're pulled in," Gavin said. "Although I haven't noticed any of his nets being cut, I've checked with other lobstermen in the area. Many of their catches have been lower than usual, as well."

"I understand there's a new lobster franchise situated up along the Canadian coast," Ed informed him, leaning back in his chair. "The Lobster Cove PD has been keeping an eye on them. Daryl Johnson says their licenses are in order. It's a young group. Apparently they all check out."

"I've contacted the Coast Guard and talked to Sinclair Bennson. Asked him to be on the lookout for any suspicious activity in the area," Gavin said. "I'll contact Daryl and share what we know. Something certainly looks fishy."

"Speaking of fishy," Sylvia interjected, "here comes our meal. No more business talk. Let's enjoy the sunshine, good food, and wonderful company."

"Here, here." Jonathan raised his glass. "I'll drink

to that."

Other than a brief moment discussing the investigation into the McClintock's lobster decline, making her hold her breath, hoping Bethany wouldn't mention her affair with Sebastian McClintock, the meal passed quickly without incident. She thoroughly enjoyed Sylvia and Jonathan's company. And even Bethany's demeanor was bright and cheery today. Still Nora was relieved when the meal came to an end, and Ed had to get back to work, which broke up the gathering. She was about to say her goodbyes when Gavin placed his hand on her shoulder and waylaid her. She found the thoughtful look on his face puzzling and once again felt a faint tingling at his touch.

"We're going out on the yacht this afternoon. Join us?" Gavin suggested.

Not a good idea to spend more time outside office hours with him, and his family, in such intimate gatherings. Going out on his boat for business was one thing. This invitation was too personal. As much as she'd love to enjoy an afternoon at sea today, she needed to keep their relationship on a business level. Thankfully she had a ready excuse to fall back on. She had already accepted Jackie's barbeque invitation.

"I'd love to, but I've been invited to my friend and her family's for the evening. Thanks for the offer. Perhaps another time?"

"I'll be out of the office most of the week. Don't forget the end of season soccer get-together is Friday night." He smiled, squeezed her shoulders, his hands firm, strong. His eyes held her in place for far too long to be comfortable. His lips lifted to one side. Those dimples… She wished she knew what he was thinking.

She wanted to lean into him and find out if it was the same thing she was thinking. Wondering what it would be like if their lips did meet.

****

As soon as she entered the house, shut the front door, and was in the process of taking her jacket off, the phone rang. Jackie. It had to be Jackie. The woman had a sixth sense.

She read the caller ID and shook her head, then lifted the receiver.

"I didn't want to use your cell phone in case you were otherwise involved with Mr. Gorgeous." Jackie didn't give her a chance to say hello. "So I took the chance you'd be home. It's late. Where have you been?"

"It's not late, and as you know, the family invited me to join them at Mariner's for lunch. It was all very innocent. So how was your whale-watching excursion?"

"You're changing the subject, girlfriend, and I want details."

"Nothing to report."

"Don't believe you."

"Jackie, Gavin is my boss. I'm not going to do anything to mess up my employment. I need the job if I want to move on without falling on my face again. This afternoon at the park, Eugenia McClintock's speech floored me, yet it gave me hope. I don't want to screw that up. It was as if she gave me a key to Lobster Cove while the whole town was watching."

"Awesome. And long overdue."

"I know. It's a good beginning. It's a first step in helping me start my own business."

"But Mr. Gavin Redmond isn't married. And as far as I'm aware, he isn't attached. And he's a war hero. I say go for it."

"I'm not looking for a relationship. I need to get my life in order before I can even contemplate a relationship. I want to make it on my own. Start my own accounting business. It's called earning your way in life. I don't want to have to depend on a man, Jackie."

"I know you are an honest person. I hope others can see the real you, too. Including Mr. Redmond. By the way, are you coming over tonight? Brad's putting the ribs on the grill as we speak."

"Give me a minute. I stopped home to change my clothes and grab a sweater."

"Great. See you soon."

Darn it. Jackie was sure to pounce on her the minute she arrived. Her friend had a way of grilling that had nothing to do with barbecuing.

****

Gavin sat back in the cushioned chair on the back of the family yacht and gazed across the wide expanse of the ocean, drink in hand, as his family settled in around him. What the hell was wrong with him? Kissing Nora Spears had been a mistake. It might have been a simple peck on the cheek, but after the urge to hold her while they were at the cemetery the other day, the emotions had intensified. It may have been a quick kiss, but once his lips touched her soft skin, he'd wanted more. Much more. He'd wanted to kiss her on the lips today. See if she responded the way he imagined, hoped, she would. Seeing her at the office everyday had his thoughts wandering, wanting to wrap his arms around her and hold her against his aching body.

Hell, hiring her had been a mistake.

Hell's bells, it'd been too long since he'd held a woman in his arms, and despite Beth's constant arranging meetings with women, girls, really, although tempting at times, he'd abstained. He was too busy rebuilding the family business. Too emotionally scarred by Celina's death. He hadn't been there for her in the beginning, hadn't given his all in their relationship. He wasn't capable of giving his all to any relationship in order to make it worthwhile. He wasn't worthy of loving again.

As for Nora Spears? She was off limits. He wasn't into office relationships. They never ended well. Although he'd detected a vibe coming from her, which led him to believe she was interested in him, he couldn't let it get personal. Nora was an ideal employee, he didn't want to lose her because he couldn't control his hormones while she was in the same room. Good thing he was out of the office investigating cases and meeting with clients a good portion of the time. And as for her working closely with the McClintocks? Eugenia McClintock had released the stigma of Nora's connection from the equation. He hadn't been worried about it to begin with. As far as he was concerned, after finding out the facts, Nora had been the victim.

It was providence that she wasn't able to join them this afternoon. His mother would have gotten the wrong impression of their relationship. It was strictly business—nothing more.

He probably shouldn't have invited her to the

soccer bash on Friday.

"So, dear brother, what has you so deep in contemplations? Not Ms. Spears, I hope," Bethany asked as she sat in the cushioned seat next to him, a glass of wine in one hand and a *Home Beautiful* magazine in the other.

"None of your business. Just relaxing. How about you? Still working on redecorating your home?"

Not only had Beth been working on his love life this past year, she'd been trying to get him to redecorate his home along with her own house. She thought putting a new face on his home would help him get over his wife's death faster, change things up in an effort to drive her memory out of his home. He hadn't wanted to change a thing. Celina had had excellent taste. There was no reason to destroy the artistic ambiance she had created, turning a house into a home.

"Ed thinks we should install a therapeutic hot tub off the family room. Set up the exercise area he's been talking about for so long."

"I'm sure he could use it after his daily shift on the force."

"What about you? You could use some relaxing, too. Although, I think you could do with a party-type hot tub."

"Don't go there. I'm not looking to entertain anyone in a hot tub, let alone a 'party.' I'm too old for that sort of activity. Besides, I have the bay and the ocean right on my doorstep. I have enough water in my work day."

"You're hiding yourself in your work. You need to let go, move on. Why won't you at least get out more? Have some fun? See other people?"

"I see people. I meet with clients, have lunch with them, and go out on their boats."

"That's not what I mean, and you know it. I'm talking about women. Dating. Getting back in the game. Don't you want to get married again, have a family?"

"Haven't thought about it." Nora's face popped into his mental vision. He blinked to dispel the image.

"It's time you did. You're in your prime. Still time to find someone, have a kid or two."

"Bethany, you're overstepping. You know how I feel about kids."

"Yes. You love them. I know you were disappointed when you discovered Celina wasn't able to have kids."

"I wasn't disappointed. I loved Celina regardless of whether or not she could have babies. Had she not been so ill, we would have adopted. Besides, I'm happy working with the Wounded Warriors and their families and children. Especially helping to coach soccer."

"It's not the same, and you know it."

"It's rewarding coaching and watching the young ones kick a soccer ball around the field or swing a bat. I enjoy spending time with them while their parents, who aren't able to get in on the action, are at least able to support them by showing up and watching from the bench when they can. What about you?" He turned the tables on her, taking the focus away from him. "Don't you want a family? A couple of kids of your own?"

"We're working on it."

Beth's smile spread across her face. Gavin was sure her eyes sparkled behind her sunglasses.

"How does Ed feel?"

"He's enjoying working on it as much as I am."

"More information than I need to know."

"I'm due for a checkup next week. Fingers crossed we're already in the family way. But don't mention a word of it to Mom. I want to be the one to surprise her if it's positive. She'll be tickled, I know."

"Mum's the word."

Chapter Nine

The fire hall parking lot was full to overflowing Friday night as Nora pulled in. She circled the station, looking for a place to park. Not finding any, she almost changed her mind and decided not to attend the end of season soccer picnic. But as she pulled out onto Main Street, she found a spot, pulled in, and parked before she had a chance to change her mind.

Smoke from the barbeque pit circled overhead and filled the air with the spicy aroma of roasted chicken as she made her way to the side lawn. Kids were in the field playing soccer, while farther over others were playing volleyball. Several adults were engaged in a game of horseshoes. She walked past a long row of tables already piled high with an assortment of salads, fruits, vegetables, and desserts undercover of the pavilion. A white party tent was set up next to the pavilion where she spotted Jackie and a few of the other mothers setting tables.

"What can I do to help?" she asked as she joined Jackie.

"Just putting the finishing touches on the tables. The others have the food tables ready to go as soon as the chicken comes off the grill. Hang out and relax. Even the kids are already having a ball—pardon the pun."

"There must be something I can do. You know me.

I can't sit still for long."

"Why don't you check on the drinks, see if Tasha needs help making more lemonade? The kids will be thirsty after running all over the field. Or you can go see how the chicken is coming. I believe Gavin is one of the men grilling."

"Don't start," Nora chided Jackie.

"What? He did invite you, right?"

"Not in the way you mean. He suggested I come. I wouldn't have come if it weren't for you and the boys."

"You can believe that if you want to, but I know better. Don't look now, but I think he just spotted you. If that smile on his face means anything, he's happy you came."

Nora tried not to be obvious as she looked toward the barbeque pit. Sure enough, Gavin was smiling at her. He nodded in acknowledgement and then went back to tending the chicken. His smile curled her toes. Wearing a white bib apron and oversize oven mitts clear up to his elbows, he assisted Brad in turning the racks. He looked every bit as domestic as the others. And handsome as all get-out.

Jackie nudged her shoulder and smiled.

"Stop it," Nora chided again, then turned and made her way over to the pavilion where Natasha was lining up cups of lemonade for the kids.

Half an hour later, someone blew a whistle, and the kids stampeded toward the food. Nora waited for the line to dwindle before filling her plate and joining Jackie and Brad under the tent.

"Where are the boys?" she asked.

"Eating with their friends. A few of them decided to go sit over next to the bay and enjoy the sunshine."

"And to get away from the adults, I'm sure," Brad said.

"Mind if I join you?" a deep, sexy voice asked. Gavin stood next to her, laid his plate on the table, and pulled out a chair. He sat, not waiting for her answer.

She kept her eyes on her plate. She wasn't going to look up at Jackie. She knew she'd see an I-told-you-so grin on her friend's face.

"Glad you decided to come today," Gavin said, lifting his glass of lemonade and taking a hearty drink.

"It's great to see all the kids having fun regardless of whose team they're on, and who won more games."

"They're a great bunch of kids," he said before taking a bite out of his chicken, then licking his fingers.

"I second that," Brad said. "Although I might be a bit partial to my boys."

"A bit?" Jackie laughed. "What an understatement."

Nora enjoyed their banter. She'd always envied Jackie her family life, a loving husband and two adorable yet energetic boys. An only child, she'd always dreamed of having children one day. She had come to the conclusion it wasn't going to happen anytime soon. Instead, she had concentrated on her career.

"They're great boys," Gavin joined the conversation. "I enjoy working with them."

"You must love to work with kids," Jackie said. "One or two at a time is a handful. Working with a whole team of them at the same time must be exhausting."

"Building on the budding adults of tomorrow can be rewarding. I enjoy their enthusiasm, dedication, and teamwork."

"In other words, you love kids." Jackie looked over at Nora and smiled.

She was pretty sure Gavin was looking at her from the corners of his eyes. The fact they both loved kids and neither of them had any children yet didn't go unnoticed but thankfully remained unspoken. Nora's heart beat at a rapid pace. If they didn't change the subject within the next few minutes, she was going to find some excuse to leave the table.

"This chicken is delicious, even if I do say so myself," Brad said. "Slaving over those hot grills paid off."

"You always do a mean barbeque," Jackie agreed and nudged him with her shoulder.

"It is delicious," Nora, finally able to speak, agreed, licking sauce from her fingers. "You guys must have gotten up pretty early to get the grills going."

"Actually, the firemen were here early and got the coals going for us," Gavin said. "A few of the soccer parents are volunteer firemen, so they pitched in, too."

"Don't forget their wives are in the auxiliary and coordinated all the food," Jackie added. "It's a community effort. It's what I love about small communities like Lobster Cove."

Nora was beginning to feel a part of the community, thanks to Eugenia McClintock's declaration the other day. And now, being accepted at today's picnic, she was hopeful things were changing for the better.

Gavin and Brad were in deep conversation as they continued to dig in to their meal. Without warning, Gavin wound his arm over the back of her chair. She stiffened as his fingers began fondling her hair. Was he aware of what he was doing? Jackie's raised eyebrow, with her I-told-you-so look, made her insides squirm. The way her face warmed, she was sure she must have turned beet red.

She leaned forward to disengage from his erotic touch. His hand slid down her back, then rested on the table in front of him as if nothing had happened. Thankfully, it was at that moment Jackie's boys ran between the tables, laughing with excitement when they reached their parents' side.

****

Gavin wasn't even sure what he and Brad had been discussing. Something about helping Nora move. Which suddenly brought him up short. Had Brad suggested he help out? Of course he would, but before he could reply and find out what the plan was, Timmy and Cody were begging them all to play ball.

"You men go ahead," Jackie said, waving them off with her hand. "Nora and I will help clean up."

"We'll catch up later." Gavin stood, needing to distance himself in order to figure out what was going on between him and Nora.

And what the hell was he doing touching her? Running his fingers through her silky soft, sexy hair, wondering what it would be like to hold her and…oh, my God, kiss her for real?

Playing ball with the kids and their parents took his mind off Nora Spears and the warm feelings starting to drive his insides to mush. However, the minute playtime ended and he went back to look for her, in anticipation of possibly continuing their evening together, his disappointment intensified when he discovered she had already left.

****

About to cart a box of clothes out to the car Saturday morning, Nora hesitated on the front steps as Gavin pulled into the driveway. He drew to a stop next to her car with a small flatbed trailer attached to his pickup truck. He shut the motor off, jumped out, and shut the door.

"What are you doing here?" she asked, holding the box against her hip.

He looked sexy in his dark blue denims and white turtleneck. The smile on his face had her heart doing cartwheels. Until she looked over his shoulder and saw Chuck peering through his window, his hand holding the curtain to the side, not even trying to be inconspicuous. The sleazy grin on his face made her want to throw something at him. At least he was staying inside and hadn't offered his assistance yet.

"I'm here to lend a hand. We talked about it at the picnic last night," Gavin said as he approached her. "Here, give me the box, then you can show me what else needs to be moved."

Brad and Jackie had discussed helping her, but for the life of her, she didn't recall Gavin offering to lend a hand. Had she been so discombobulated with him running his fingers through her hair that she hadn't heard him offer to help?

"There really isn't much to be moved. Jackie is finishing packing up the kitchen. Brad had to take the boys to their grandmother's." She handed him the box. "There really isn't much more to be done."

"Then it should be a snap to get things on the trailer. Let me get this loaded, and then you can show me what else you need help with."

"I have it all under control."

"I'm sure you do," he said, a smile in his voice as he carried the box to the trailer and returned. "How many trips you plan on making?"

"As I said, there isn't much to move. With your trailer, I'm sure it will be a single trip."

"Guess I got here in time, then. Lead on."

She put her hands on her hips, staring at him as he walked past her toward the front steps. He turned when he reached the front door, raised his eyebrows, and gave her a devilish grin that lit up his entire face.

Those dimples. Good Lord, she was in trouble.

"Come on, Nora. I'm here. Might as well lend a hand. You've helped me out a lot at the office. It's the least I can do."

"You've paid me to work at the office. It's not the same thing, and you know it."

"Okay, so I've been a bit preoccupied lately with the clients. I haven't been in the office much the past few days. Thought we could spend more time together this weekend. Get to know each other better."

What? What was he trying to say? Sure, there had been moments when she'd though he was interested in her, but then he'd be aloof and act as if she didn't exist. She had been getting mixed messages and had determined not to delve into her own feelings.

"Let's get inside away from your nosey neighbor's prying eyes."

She looked over her shoulder and spotted Chuck standing in his doorway, looking as if he was about to head their way. "Oh, Lord. That's all I need." Resigned, she turned, her shoulder bumping against Gavin's solid chest. She missed a step and tripped. Gavin gripped her arms before she fell, his touch zinging her insides clear down to her toes.

"Steady. Can't have you tripping up the steps before we get the job done."

"Sorry. I was in a hurry to get inside the house before Chuck decided to join us."

"Does he bother you much?"

"As often as he can. One of the main reasons I'm moving. Should have done it months ago, but it was a matter of finances."

She led him inside, to a small room to the right of the foyer. Boxes were already packed and stacked up against a wall.

"Organized as usual, I see. I'll carry these out while you check on Jackie. See if she needs any help."

"Bossy much?"

"Takes one to know one. What's the plan for lunch? My treat."

She didn't respond and instead left him to move boxes while she went to see how Jackie was doing in the kitchen.

"So. Gavin Redmond is here. I couldn't help but overhear you two talking."

"Admit it, you eavesdropped."

"Sure. You'd do the same. By the way, I got a call from Brad. One of the boys got hurt on the playground, so I have to take him to the walk-in. Think you can manage on your own now that backup has arrived?" Her friend's smile was overbright.

"What? You're leaving me alone with him?"

"What's the big deal? You're alone with him at work most of the day. How is this any different?"

"You know perfectly well what the difference is."

"Yep. And I'm jumping ship. You don't need me at this point. I've got everything in boxes except for a few essentials you'll need before you leave this place for good. You can handle the rest. Just don't pass up any golden opportunities with Mr. Redmond."

"Jackie…"

"Good luck. Call me. I want details."

"You always want details."

"I'm hoping they're good ones this time. I want you to be happy."

"Jackie…"

"See ya. Bye."

She heard Jackie talking to Gavin as she left the house. Nora crossed her fingers and hoped Jackie wasn't playing matchmaker.

Chapter Ten

Steaming coffee in hand, French vanilla aroma trailing behind her, Nora sat at her desk, ready to start the day Monday morning. Her mind, however, was on Gavin and the embrace they had shared at her new home, on Saturday. She'd showed him around the house after he'd brought in the rest of the boxes from his trailer. He'd seemed genuinely interested and pleased with her choice of houses. Still, it'd been a surprise when they returned to the front room and were looking out the window at the view of Lobster Cove, and he'd wrapped his arms around her and hugged her to him. And proceeded to kiss her on her cheek. A kiss that had his lips covering hers in an all-consuming embrace. Her heart had raced, and her knees about gave out. It had been way more than a surprise. It had been a spine-tingling experience that left her speechless. And falling head over heels for Gavin Redmond.

Now, deep in thought, not for the first time, she was brought out of her erotic contemplations when the bell over the door rang. She turned to find a petite blonde had entered and walked right up to her desk, a broad smile on her perfectly made-up face.

Had Bethany sent yet another blonde bimbo to entice Gavin?

The woman standing in front of her really didn't look like any of the other girls Bethany had sent

Gavin's way. About five-three, with straight hair cut short around her ears, she was stylishly but decorously dressed in navy slacks and a sleeveless, white eyelet blouse.

"Is Gavin in?" she asked, her hand clutching a small beige purse with fingernails polished a bright mauve lacquer. "He told me to meet him here this morning." Her voice was smooth, well spoken. And she obviously had already met Gavin if he'd invited her to his workplace. Perhaps a client?

"I'm sorry, he's not in yet. Can I help with something?"

"No, thanks. I'll wait over here on the settee. He did say he might be a few minutes late."

"Would you like a cup of coffee while you wait?"

"That sounds lovely."

Nora rose to get the woman a coffee.

"No, no. Don't let me bother you. I know where the kitchenette is. I can help myself."

Nora sat. Checked Gavin's calendar as the young woman went to get a coffee. Nothing! No meetings scheduled for the day.

The bell over the door tinkled again, and this time Gavin walked in dressed in a business suit. Her heart skipped a beat. He was more devastatingly handsome all dressed up than he had been when he helped her move—when he had kissed her!

"Morning." He nodded in her direction, his usual warm greeting missing, his professional tone a surprise. "I'm expecting a visitor this morning. Gwendolyn Rose. Ring me when she arrives."

"She's already here. In the kitchen getting a coffee."

She watched his face light up, a smile spread across his face. Her happy thoughts plummeted. The woman was obviously more than a business associate or special friend.

"I'll take it from here," Gavin assured her as he headed toward the alcove. "By the way, I'll be out of the office the rest of the day. Hold all my calls."

She watched, open mouthed, as Gavin almost sprinted to the kitchen to meet his guest. After listening to an excited welcome from Gwendolyn Rose coming from the kitchenette, the following silence had her imagination in overdrive.

Were they kissing?

Their footsteps echoed down the hall as did Gwendolyn's warm laughter. Both grated on her nerves. Gavin's office door opened and then clicked shut. There obviously was something going on between Gavin and his visitor. His sudden business-like formal tone as he'd addressed her on his way to meet his "visitor" was more than telling. Oh, my God. She'd been such a fool to think Gavin's kisses and his attention to her the past few days indicated he was romantically interested in her. Had she been firmly put in her place as nothing more than the office employee she was? His previous warm attitude toward her was definitely lacking.

What did she expect? She'd known from the start she was no match for Gavin Redmond. And after meeting Gwendolyn Rose, she was no competition for the woman ensconced behind closed doors in Gavin's office.

And in his arms?

She plunked down in her chair behind her desk and

blankly stared at nothing as she pondered her situation. She liked working for Gavin. More than liked, actually, she loved it. It was diverse enough not to be boring on a day-to-day basis. And yes, the money was a big incentive. She needed this job. Leaving right now was not an option. But could she continue working for him knowing her feelings for him had developed into something more than friendly affection? Seeing him on a daily basis knowing he was in a relationship with someone else?

When had she fallen head over heels in love with Gavin Redmond?

She would have to suck it up and keep her feelings for him to herself.

Or start looking for another job.

She watched with a heavy heart as Gavin and Ms. Rose strolled past her desk arm in arm and left the building. She couldn't contain the deep sigh escaping between her tight lips once they shut the door behind them without a single look her way or a simple goodbye.

The afternoon dragged. She rubbed her temples, took several deep breaths, and did a few neck and shoulder exercises to relieve the tension. It'd been quiet in the office most of the day with an hour left before closing. Deciding to call it a day, she straightened her desk, shut the computer off, then tidied the kitchen and unplugged the coffee maker. Taking another fortifying breath, she retrieved her purse and lightweight jacket and stepped out into the bright afternoon sunshine. She locked the door behind her and headed for home.

As soon as she arrived, she spotted Chuck and practically ran inside, not wanting to encounter her landlord. She entered, locked the door, and walked through the empty house to the kitchen. After making a cup of tea, she grabbed her phone and went out on the back deck. She settled in the Adirondack chair and dialed Jackie's number.

"Oh, my gaud, Jackie, he has a girlfriend. Her name is Gwendolyn Rose. She's beautiful."

The late afternoon breeze teased her hair as she talked to Jackie on the phone.

"Wow. I'm assuming you're talking about Gavin Redmond? I knew it. I knew you were smitten."

"Okay, so I have feelings for him."

"Knew it. So who is this Rose person? Her name doesn't ring a bell."

"Bethany probably set the whole thing up for them to meet again. His sister has been trying to fix him up with someone since his wife died."

"So we'll find someone for you to go out with, too. Get your mind off Mr. Redmond."

"I don't need to 'find' someone else. What am I going to do? I need this job. I just bought a house, dammit. I need the money. Don't you see? How can I continue to work for him knowing how I feel about him and knowing he is in a relationship with someone else? I don't want to be the other woman again. I don't want to be the one to cause another breakup. I'm going to have to find another job."

"How are you going to be able to afford the cottage if you leave Redmond's?"

She took a deep breath, let it out, and leaned back in her chair, staring at the deep-blue sky above. There were no answers there.

"I guess I'll have to remain at Redmond's until I

find another job. I hadn't really started looking when I landed this one. I'm sure there is something else out there for me. I'll have to hang in here a bit longer."

"Don't be too hasty. Maybe he's being polite, not wanting to hurt an old friend's feelings."

"I don't think I'll be able to see him every day knowing how I feel about him, yet knowing he's in a relationship with someone else. After my disastrous relationship with Sebastian, I'm not about to—"

"Aren't you listening? I said, maybe he's just being friendly. Maybe there isn't a relationship. Maybe his sister is behind this. Wow, girl, you've got it bad."

"I can't believe it either, but you're right. However, I'm not about to ruin another person's relationship no matter if they aren't married. I've learned my lesson."

"All the more reason to go out with other men. Brad's friend, Robert Wells, is just the guy. He's thirty-two, tall, dark, handsome as sin, and single. He's visiting from New York."

"He's not gay, is he? Why else would he be single at his age?"

"Calm down, Nora. Geesh. Rob's wife didn't happen to be a dog lover. She got tired of him spending more time with their menagerie than with her. She walked out on him three years ago. Can you believe it? Over a few dogs?"

"A few dogs?"

"What? You love dogs."

"Yes, but a menagerie? I don't know, Jackie. Let me think about it."

"No problem. So Brad and the kids and I are going to Ned's Lobster Shack for supper tonight. I promised the boys they could check out the tanks with the fresh catch of the day while we're there. Come join us."

"I love fresh lobster subs. What time? I'll meet you there."

She hung up, put her head in her hands, her elbows on the side of the chair, and closed her eyes. Damn. It was all happening too fast, closing on the cottage and moving by the end of the week. She couldn't wait to get out of Sebastian's place despite the perfect location. If it weren't for the rent and Chuck coming on to her every time she left or returned to the house, and suggesting he help her with the move, she'd love to stay right where she was. And just when she thought she was getting her emotional life back in order, she'd fallen in love with someone who was in a relationship with someone else.

Her mind buzzed to the point she was developing a major migraine. She repeated the neck rub and shoulder exercises and then went inside to get ready to meet Jackie and her family. Tomorrow would have to take care of itself. Tonight? Tonight she was going to try and relax and rethink things. Especially her feelings for Gavin Redmond.

****

"Is Beth on board yet?" Gavin asked the skipper of his family's yacht.

"No, sir. She called to say she couldn't make it. She'll talk to you later. If you and your guest are ready, I'll get this rig underway."

He cringed inwardly. Beth was up to her old tricks where Gwen was concerned. She was matchmaking again. He was going to have words with his sister when they returned.

"I'm sorry, Gavin." Gwen faked a pout, sounding

anything but sorry.

Great. He'd totally been set up.

Despite the brilliant sun and clear azure sky, his spirits dwindled. It didn't help when Gwen tucked her arm in his and led him to the wet bar along the interior wall of the enclosed solar.

"We have the afternoon to ourselves." She leaned her head sideways toward him in a sexy pose, her hip nudged him in invitation. "How about you get us a drink, and we can sit right here out of the wind. Relax. Catch up."

"Sure. What would you like?" Resigned, Gavin stepped out of her grasp and turned toward the wine rack. "I'm sure there are some local wines in stock."

"Wine sounds lovely. You choose."

He grabbed the first bottle he came to and poured the clear liquid into two long-stemmed flutes. He nodded for her to have a seat as he carried them to the round table tucked among several easy chairs. Gwen settled on the settee instead and patted the cushion next to her in invitation. Not wanting to be rude, he complied.

Gwen took the glass, raised it to meet his, and said, "To renewed friendships."

"Friendships." He sipped from his glass, hoping like hell friendship was really all she was interested in. He didn't want to hurt her feelings, but there was no way there would be anything more between them than friendship. He had to tell her, before they went any further. He saw the hope in her eyes, was lost for words, and held his tongue.

Damn it. The afternoon was going to be a disaster.

He was reluctant to leave the shelter of the solar,

but Gwen made several attempts to close the gap between them. Each time, he found excuses to shift away from her without being rude. He tried to interest her in the aquatic life out on the bay, but she didn't seem to care what was happening on the open seas on the other side of window panels. They dined on picnic food Beth had apparently prepared for them in advance. He was thankful to put the food between them on the small table in the middle of the room, and for the time it took to dine and then to clean up. He was relieved when it was finally time to turn the vessel around and head back to the dock. He had to set Gwen straight, let her down as easy as possible. He hoped he hadn't left it too late.

He stood at the bar, empty glasses in hand, when Gwen wrapped her arms around his back and snuggled in close. Her head rested between his shoulder blades. He stiffened.

"Mmmm. I've been waiting to hold you since we got on board, Gav. Don't tell me you haven't wanted to do the same. Haven't you felt the vibes between us, too?"

Her sexy voice made him cringe. Damn, he had left it too late. He hung his head, shifted, and turned smack-dab into her arms. He didn't see the kiss coming, hadn't expected it, but should have. There were no feelings, no emotions coursing through his body when her lips met his. It was all wrong. It was like kissing his sister. He grasped her shoulders and nudged her aside. Her closed eyes popped open. He saw the confusion in her beautiful, emotion-filled blue eyes. Double damn. She wasn't making this easy.

"Listen, Gwen. I think we need to talk about this."

He pointed his finger between the two of them. "Us."

"I know. Don't you feel it, too?"

Good Lord, her face was filled with sensual bliss from the kiss he hadn't expected or wanted.

"Let's sit down and discuss it. There is something you should know."

"Oh, Gav. I've missed you these last few years." She all but swooned.

"Sit. And listen to me, please."

"Oh. Okay." She turned and sashayed all the way back to the settee.

When she turned and spotted him still standing across the room, her mouth dropped opened in confusion. Her eyes lowered as the hope in them for the anticipated intimate afternoon was replaced with disappointment. She was finally getting the picture. Hoping to let her down easy, he sat in the chair opposite her, rubbed his fingers across his chin, and decided to spit it out.

"I'm sorry if you're getting the wrong impression, Gwen. But I'm not ready for a relationship. I'm pretty sure my sister is behind this *set-up*. And it isn't fair to you—or me."

"I don't understand." Her eyes wide, she sat up, shoulders pulled back, ready to defend her resolve that they did have a relationship.

"You know Bethany was supposed to join us today, right?"

"Well, yes. But that doesn't have anything to do with us."

"You're right, Gwendolyn, because there really is nothing between us, there is no us, just friendship. That's all it ever was, all it will ever be. I'm sorry, I don't know how else to put this, but I need to be frank. I don't love you, and I'm not looking for a fling of any kind. I've told Bethany a number of times, but she doesn't listen."

He watched Gwen stand and rush to the window at the back of the solar. Shit! He hoped she wasn't going to cry. He hated tears. He stood, and in slow motion, made his way to her side.

"I'm sorry," he whispered. "I didn't mean to hurt you."

"At least you were honest. I can't believe I've fallen for Bethany's ploy. Again."

"Yes, well, she can be a handful when it comes to matters of the heart. If it makes you feel any better, you aren't the first one I've had to turn down. Honestly, Gwen, you deserve better. Stop living in Bethany's romantic world of fairy tales and find your own heart's desire."

"What makes you think you aren't mine?"

"I never was. Bethany wanted us to be each other's heart's desire because she wanted us to find the same happiness she's found with Ed."

****

The sun shifted west across another clear brilliant sky as Gavin made his way up Main Street, leaving Bar Harbor's active wharf behind. Hands in pockets, he pondered the day's events spent with Gwen on Frenchman Bay. Seeing her again after all this time warmed his insides as he thought about the final hug and goodbye kiss they'd exchanged on the yacht an hour ago. At least they had parted as friends. Bethany's college friend had been like part of the family back in the day. He knew his sister had hopes he and

Gwendolyn would become more than friends. As much as Gavin had adored Gwendolyn then, she wasn't the one for him. Now? Now he was going to have to speak to Bethany and tell her to stop interfering in his love life.

And Gwendolyn's.

He turned the corner of Main and Cottage and headed back to the office in anticipation of seeing Nora. He needed to apologize to her. He'd been curt to her this morning. He hadn't meant to be, but his emotions were going haywire where she was concerned. He didn't know where their relationship was headed. True, he was growing more than fond of her. But he was knee-deep in trying to rebuild the family business, a time-consuming job. He didn't have time for a relationship of any kind.

Still, he couldn't stop thinking about how she had felt in his arms, her soft skin, and that kiss last night. And her ardent response.

She was as attracted to him as he was to her.

About to enter the office, he turned the handle, but the door remained shut. Locked! He checked his watch and then retrieved his building keys, unlocked the door, entered, and stopped short. The reception area was dark. Where was Nora?

Chapter Eleven

It wasn't closing time, so where the hell was Nora? Had she had an emergency and had to leave?

He searched her desk for a note. Nothing! His concern was overshadowed by a niggling suspicion that perhaps Nora's absence might have something to do with Gwendolyn showing up and him spending the day with her. Especially after the kiss they had shared last night. His heart thumped in his chest just thinking about the possibility of her being upset with him to the point she felt she had to leave the office early. Hopefully, she hadn't quit.

Crap! This was exactly why he had no time for a relationship, let alone an office relationship.

He trekked to his lab but found no release in checking his latest results on the samples he'd taken earlier in the week. As it stood, he had no answers for the McClintock Fisheries clamoring for results. He picked up the phone and put a call in to the Lobster Cove Coast Guard. Perhaps they had come up with a few leads of their own this past week.

Petty Officer Calla Hutchins picked up on the first ring.

"Hello, Officer Hutchins, Gavin Redmond here. Does Officer Bennson have any new information to share in regards to the McClintock case?"

"We've been keeping a close watch on a new

fishing operation off the coast of Canada. They're small, but they seem to be doing a stroke of business. How about you? Have you uncovered any new leads on your end?"

"Possibly. I discovered a knife with an interesting looking emblem where one of the McClintock's nets was cut. I've been trying to identify the markings but haven't come up with anything yet."

"Any fingerprints?"

"Negative. Not surprising, but the markings on the knife look foreign. I'm thinking Norwegian, at least Scandinavian."

"Bring it in. We have a file we can search. We can see if it matches one from our previous cases."

"I can be there in about an hour. Will that work for you?"

"I'll be here. I'll have a few files open so we can go over them together."

"Great. See you soon."

He hung up, retrieved the box with the knife, locked the office for the night, and headed for Lobster Cove. His mind more on Nora Spears and why she had left early than on the McClintock case.

****

"You wicked friend," Nora whispered to Jackie the first chance she got after meeting her at Ned's Lobster Shack. "I told you I didn't want to be set up with Robert Wells."

"You said you'd think about it. And if I know you, you wouldn't give it a single thought."

She shouldn't have been surprised when she walked into Ned's to find the tall, dark, and handsome friend of Brad's smiling at her as if they were already a twosome. He was congenial, warm, friendly, and politely annoying to the point he was too cloying. Too soon. Thankfully, he seemed to take her cold shoulder in stride and backed off, retreating with Brad and the boys to check out the fish tanks on the opposite side of the room.

"He's perfect," Jackie continued, watching the men cross to the tanks.

"So I see. However, I'm not interested, Jackie."

She glanced at Robert. He was handsome with sparkling eyes to match his warm smile. But his interest in a long-term relationship wasn't there. Nor was hers.

"You know love can't be turned on or off at will, Jackie. It will take time to find someone. In the meantime, I don't need a hook-up, blind date, or friend of a friend. Robert seems like a nice person. If he really is looking for someone, he needs to not come on so strong so soon to every woman he meets for the first time."

"He's only in town for a couple of days." Jackie sipped from her tall frosted glass and leaned forward. "The least you can do is go out with him and keep him company."

Nora leaned forward and whispered across the table. "I can't believe you're asking me to go there. No! The answer is no, Jackie. I don't want to encourage him. Let it go."

"Okay. At least stay a little longer and enjoy the evening. What can it hurt?" Jackie gave in with a deep sigh.

"Another iced tea and then I need to go home and finish packing, more like sorting through the last-minute items. I can't wait to get totally moved in this weekend."

"Need any help?" Jackie's grin and raised eyebrows were telling.

"Don't you even suggest asking Brad and Robert to help."

"Why not let us help?"

"I can handle this part on my own. We've got most of my things moved, thanks to Gavin. If I need help, I'll let you know."

No way she wanted to enlist Robert's help. It would only encourage him.

Thankfully Timmy and Cody rushed back to the table, breaking the tension with their excitement at seeing all the live fish in the tanks. Brad and Robert followed more sedately.

"Mom, you should see the big claws on the giant lobster in the big tank. They were this big." Timmy's excitement, as he held up his arms and stretched them out either side to indicate the size of the lobster, brought a smile to everyone's faces. The two boys talked nonstop as they sat down on either side of Jackie.

Robert ordered a new round of drinks for everyone, soda for the boys, then proceeded to sit down next to her. His leg bumped against hers as he leaned in toward her. She ignored the words he whispered in her ear, as she looked up and spotted Gavin entering the eatery.

Their eyes met. Her heart skipped a beat. Like a tennis match, Gavin's eyes swiveled from hers to Robert's and back again. He raised his left eyebrow in question. What? He had the nerve to question her? What was it to him if she was seeing someone? After all, he'd spent the day with Gwendolyn Rose.

She raised her own eyebrow, daring him to

question her. He nodded, then walked past the table to the other side of the room to place his order. Seeing Gavin tonight and being hurt by his actions had only made things more complicated. Oh, Lordy, how was she going to face him in the morning?

Still, she was drawn to his tall, fit physique—his dark hair brushed back from his face as he waited in line to order his takeaway meal. He was wearing a white, button-down, cotton shirt with rolled-up sleeves and a pair of black slacks as if he were on his way to or from an important meeting. Hands down, he was way more appealing than Robert. Just thinking about the kiss, his light, caring touch turned hot, had her sweating. Jackie was right; she had it bad. If she knew what was good for her, she'd cut and run.

Maybe she should go out with Robert. Then again, she really didn't want to lead Robert on. She wasn't looking for a one-night stand.

Her attention was once again drawn into the boys' chatter. When she looked up again, Gavin was gone.

****

Gavin ordered a lobster sub and a coffee to go and then hightailed it out of Ned's. He found a bench along the pier and sat staring out across Frenchman Bay. The fact Nora might be in a relationship hadn't crossed his mind, especially after their kiss last night. Seeing her with the man who was almost sitting in her lap had been a shock. Recalling what little he really knew about her had him rethinking the rumors his sister had shared with him. Were they true? She'd been working for him for several weeks and had given no indication she was in a relationship. He hadn't seen her with another man in all that time, and if she was in a relationship, why had she joined him and his family for lunch on Monday? Even with the events at the Memorial Day celebration, it was hard for him to believe the gossip. He wasn't one to believe everything he heard and only half of what he'd seen. Yet for some reason, suddenly seeing Nora enjoying herself with another man rubbed him the wrong way. Especially after their shared kiss. He couldn't get that kiss out of his mind. He thought for sure they were…

Hell! He had more pressing matters to think about, like discovering who was trying to put the McClintocks out of business and catching the culprits red-handed.

McClintock's Fisheries were spread out to the north along Lobster Cove's inlet. Activity on this dock was busy as trawlers lined up, docking for the evening. He wasn't looking forward to talking to Colman Baker, especially as he was about to inform him what he had found out. McClintock's nets had been cut, and the markings on the knife he'd found indicated several of the young men working for him had knives and tats with the same markings. Calla Hutchins had confirmed the connection. The Coast Guard had been keeping an eye on the men and had already called in Homeland Security.

He swallowed the last bit of his lobster roll, crumpled the wrapper, drained the rest of his coffee, and tossed both in the trash receptacle on his way back down the dock to Coleman Baker's office. The breeze off the bay was invigorating this time of year, and the sun was slowly shifting toward the west, his sunglasses deflecting the bright rays. The scent of seaweed, oysters, and mussels along the New England shoreline and the sound of water slapping against the pier was somehow relaxing. He'd grown up in the area, and being on or near the water was soothing.

Coleman Baker was waiting for him when he entered McClintock and McClintock Lobster Fisheries.

"Welcome, welcome. Have you any concrete news?" Coleman asked, as he escorted Gavin down the hall to his inner office where they could carry on their conversation in private. "Would you like a coffee?"

"No, thanks, I just finished one. Thanks for seeing me so late this evening. As you know, I stopped off at the Coast Guard and talked to Officer Hutchins. I think we might have some good news in regards to your situation."

"So give it to me straight," Coleman encouraged, as he sat at his desk, cleared his throat, and crossed his left leg over his right knee. He leaned back in his chair and took a deep breath. "I can see it really isn't good news."

Gavin also sat before replying. "You're right. I'm afraid you might have a few employees who have been helping themselves to your catch."

"What?" Coleman jumped to his feet, the chair rocking backward. "Are you serious? What makes you so sure it's McClintock's men?"

Gavin explained about the findings, the knife he'd found, the tats, the emblems, and the information Officer Hutchins had disclosed.

"Not sure what you want to do with this information, Coleman, but Officer Hutchins is ready to act if you are. They think they have enough evidence against them to proceed. It might affect you quicker than you'd like."

"I'll need to contact Hunter McClintock in Hawaii.

They're due for a business trip out here next week."

"It sounded to me as if the Coast Guard wanted to act right away."

"I'll contact Hunter. See what he thinks. Perhaps he could come sooner."

"Okay, I'll talk to Officer Hutchins again and see if she can hold off a few days. Give me a chance to do a couple more dives and check the nets and traps to gain more evidence."

"Good idea. I'll call Hunter this evening and get back with you."

"In the meantime, perhaps you can do a bit of your own sleuthing and see what employees are involved before all hell breaks loose."

****

Nora was at her desk when Gavin showed up for work the following morning. She still wasn't prepared to see him after last night's disastrous evening with Robert and the thought of Gavin having spent the day in the arms of Ms. Rose. But his tall, domineering presence as he entered the office sent her heart fluttering like a giddy teenager's. He appeared fresh from a shower. With his dark hair still damp, his crisp denims and blue, chambray, button-down shirt with rolled-up sleeves, he resembled a hot, sexy preppy.

She turned to her computer and mumbled, "Good morning." His response was spoken closer to her desk than she'd expected. She looked up to see him leaning toward her, his hands in his pockets, his eyes glued to hers.

"Can I help you with something?" A stupid question seeing as he was her boss, and she was there to serve him.

"As a matter of fact, I think we need to clear the air."

"Oh? How so?"

"I think you know."

"If it's about snubbing me last night at Ned's, there's nothing to discuss."

"I think there is. After all, we've shared a few intimate moments. And I wasn't snubbing you."

Her face warmed as she gazed into his deep ocean-blue eyes turned a stormy gray. "I don't follow. What intimate moments?"

"Don't play coy with me. You know as well as I do we have feelings for each other."

"We have?" Surprised to say the least, she stood to face him. Had he really noticed she had feelings for him? Even though she had tried to hide them? Well, except for responding to his hot kiss!

"So why didn't you tell me you were in a relationship? I would have understood. I wouldn't have made a pass at you the other day."

"What? What makes you think I'm seeing someone?"

"Last night at Ned's."

"You can't believe everything you see. You know better."

"You mean I'm wrong?"

"Yes. I was with friends. Why the twenty questions?"

"I thought we had something going between us. Guess I was wrong about that, too."

"So am I wrong about you and Ms. Rose?"

"Oh, so you were upset about Gwen yesterday? Is that why you were gone when I got back to the office?

Went out with your '*friend*?'"

Hands on hips, she shot back at him, "For your information, Mr. Redmond, I'm not about to interfere in another person's relationship, married or not. That's not who I am. Lesson learned, remember? And by the way, Robert is not my friend, he's Brad's."

"It's not who I am, either. I'm not involved with Gwendolyn, never have been. It's all in her and Bethany's heads."

Gavin reached for her and swept her into his arms. She was further startled when he covered her mouth with a long, lingering kiss. It had her body temperature boiling and threw her into a tailspin.

Without thinking, she wrapped her arms around his neck and gave in to his embrace, her desire. Just as suddenly, he let her go. Stunned, she stared at him, transfixed, as a hot, searing heat of sexual need washed over her.

"I'm not going to apologize for that kiss. I've wanted to kiss you since the first day you walked into this office."

She stepped back on shaky legs. Her knees bumped against her chair, and she sat. She shot back up and faced him, hands on hips.

"We can't do this. You're my boss. I need this job. I just bought a house. This is too sudden."

"We can work this out. I'm hardly in the office as it is." He rubbed his hand through his thick hair, then over his face. He turned away, then swung back around and reached for her again. "Look, I know you have feelings for me, otherwise you wouldn't have responded to my kiss as ardently as you did the other day and especially right now. I'm going to be honest with you. I want to see more of you, and not in a business capacity here at the office, either."

"What about your family? Bethany?" What was she thinking? It would never work.

"If you haven't figured it out yet, let me set the record straight. My family does not run my life. Does not choose who I can and can't go out with. I don't care how many girls my sister throws my way. I haven't been interested in a single one, and I've never encouraged them. Including Gwendolyn."

"I don't know, Gavin. I'm still trying to work through a lot of baggage. You know I bought a house and want to set up my own business. I don't have time to get involved in a relationship."

"You don't think I haven't baggage of my own I'm trying to work through?"

"Which means we both need more time to make sure this is what we want. Time to find out if there really is something between us. See if it's going anywhere."

Gavin hesitated, released her, and stepped back. "We can work through them together."

She remained silent for several seconds and then shook her head.

Everything was moving too fast.

"Slow down, Gavin. I have other issues to consider. And I can't continue to work for you if we are in a relationship."

"Okay. Sure," he agreed, swiping his hand through his hair. "We'll continue, status quo."

She took a step back, putting more space between them, and inhaled. "Thank you."

"Now that we got that out of the way, we do have

business to discuss. First, you should be aware Juelle and Hunter McClintock are returning to Lobster Cove. They should be here within the week. You might run into them. Coleman Baker requested their presence before the authorities confront several of their employees suspected of sabotaging the McClintocks' business in order to start their own company."

"Thanks for the warning, but I think I can handle them when and if the situation presents itself." She wasn't so sure putting a brave face on it convinced even her. Coming face to face with Juelle McClintock wasn't something she anticipated turning out well. But before Gavin could respond, she reverted to the case in point. "So you've solved the case?"

"I'm pretty sure we'll have things wrapped up once Hunter McClintock arrives. Hopefully they can set the wheels in motion and finally put an end to their dilemma. The Coast Guard is already on hand waiting, as are the local police. However, I think they're going to call in Mark Logan from Homeland Security, as it involves international waters along the Canadian border."

Mark Logan was another person she didn't look forward to dealing with should it come to that in the course of working at Redmond's. Yes, he was a decorated war hero who had attended the Memorial Day celebration alongside the other military men and women, but he was married to Katelyn Sullivan, Juelle's best friend. Thankfully Nora had been able to sidestep crossing paths with them at the Memorial Day event.

"What about you? Won't you be involved?" She focused on Gavin's part in the operation.

"No. I've done my part. I'll have to testify my findings at a later date, but the actual arrest procedure isn't part of my job." Gavin filled her in on what he and Calla Hutchins had discovered, as well as his talk with Coleman Baker.

"Are any of you in danger?"

"No. All the investigative work has been done quietly. Coleman and Calla have kept a low profile as well. The only other people who know about my research are Eric and Al. And I trust them to keep their mouths shut. Don't worry, Redmond's isn't their target."

"I wasn't worried about myself. But if you've been seen at the McClintock warehouse, you might be."

"The only person I was introduced to was Jim Sherman, McClintock's tank room manager. I didn't encounter anyone else. I appreciate you worrying about me, though. It's a positive sign." He wriggled his eyebrows, his smile disconcerting.

"It's a legitimate concern, one I would have for anyone in such a precarious situation."

"Don't downplay it, Nora. Admit you're concerned for me. And have dinner with me tonight."

"Gavin…"

"Status quo. Promise."

He raised his hand, swearing his honor, his face serious and his eyes searching.

She wanted to refuse. Seeing him outside office hours didn't feel as if it was status quo. Would it be a mistake? However, the temptation was too great to pass up.

"Status quo. This is not a date," she insisted.

"I'm too old for dating. It's dinner out, an

enjoyable evening to get to know each other better."

Still, she hesitated before finally giving in. "I'd love to. Thanks."

"Good. I'll be out of the office the rest of the day. I'm joining Eric and Al on the boat. We're going to check the McClintock nets one more time, as well as a few others in the area to be sure they aren't being affected, as well. We've been asked to take a few more water samples to make sure the waters aren't being polluted to the point of damaging the aquafer."

"The forecast is a bit iffy for this afternoon."

"No worries. Al is a great sea captain," Gavin said before he turned, pulled her into his arms for one more kiss, and then headed toward the door. He paused, hand on the handle, and faced her. "While I'm gone, call The Cliffside restaurant and make reservations for two. I'll pick you up at your place at six." And with that, he was gone.

She sat, dazed. No way could she work for him day in and day out, anticipating his kisses, his touch, and his handsome good looks. And longing for more. Besides, she wasn't about to be beholden to any man for her livelihood. Once she got established in her new home, she was going to set up her own accounting business. She'd longed to do so the past few years. How would Gavin feel about her wanting to set up her own business? What impact would it have on their relationship?

She picked up the phone and called the restaurant to make their reservations. She was further stunned with the restaurant he'd chosen for them to dine. The Cliffside was a fancy, upscale establishment. Out-of-her-league-high-class, it touted pristine white tablecloths, imported china, crystal, and real silver, not to mention lit candles on every table with subdued lighting and soft dinner music in the background. The waiters were dressed in black slacks with starched white shirts and carried crisp linen towels over their arms. And they served the best surf and turf in town. It was a romantic setting, a place Sebastian had never taken her. She was going to have to scrounge through her wardrobe to see if she had something appropriate to wear, it had been a long time since she'd dressed up for a fancy occasion.

So much for status quo.

****

Nora spent the rest of the morning concentrating on posting journal entries, setting up meetings with Gavin's clients around Bar Harbor and Lobster Cove, and updating the company's website. By lunchtime, she was ready for a break. She slipped into her sneakers, grabbed her lightweight white nautical jacket, slung her purse over her shoulder, and closed the office. A low group of clouds drifted in over Bar Harbor as she made her way toward the docks for lunch. Despite the temptation to indulge in the delicious, fresh seafood available on the wharf, she decided to save her appetite for dinner with Gavin and settled for a quick pick-up side order of clam chowder and a roll at the lobster pound. She found an empty seat at a nearby picnic table and settled in to enjoy her lunch.

It didn't take long for a breeze swirling around the harbor to turn into a strong wind as dark clouds rolled in over the bay. White frothy waves bounced against the boats tied up at the docks, causing them to bob in place. She looked out over the bay and decided it was time to return to the office before the rain started.

It wasn't unusual for the weather to turn on a dime around the coast. Yet no one along the wharf appeared concerned. Hopefully this wasn't going to be one of those torrential storms that had escaped detection on the weatherman's radar.

She quickly finished her chowder, returned her tray, zipped up her jacket, and headed back to the office. She was halfway back to Redmond's when the rain started in earnest and quickly became a steady, heavy downpour. The steam and fog soon obliterated the area surrounding the harbor. She pulled the hood over her head and picked up her pace. By the time she walked several blocks and turned the lock in the office door, she was soaked and glad to be out of the storm. She shook the rain from her jacket, hung it on the coat rack in the corner, slipped out of her wet sneakers, and headed to the kitchen for a coffee.

And then it hit her. Oh, my God. Gavin was out on his boat in the storm.

She reached for a vanilla-flavored coffee pod and inserted it in the coffee maker. The hiss of the machine as it pushed water through the pod into her cup only added to her anxiety as memories of Sebastian's accident had her hands shaking. Regardless of how competent Gavin's skipper was, she hoped he was smart enough to bring his rig back into port and get out of the storm.

She prepared her coffee with an extra dollop of half and half and carried it back to her desk. She sat, and ignoring her coffee, lowered her head in her hands. Was Gavin safe? Would anyone call her if something went wrong? No one had called her when Sebastian was taken to the hospital after the Coast Guard had rescued him. But once she'd learned of his accident and she found out where they had taken him, she'd gone to the hospital in hopes of seeing him. She'd wanted to make sure he was okay. But he hadn't been okay. And she wasn't able to see him, let alone talk to him. Except for a brief undetected moment while she witnessed his wife sitting next to him in his hospital bed in a dimly lit ICU unit, she hadn't had a chance to be the one by his side. She hadn't been there for him. Juelle had been the one holding his limp hand. His eyes had been closed, and beneath his fisherman's tan was nothing but a pale reflection of the adventuresome man he'd once been. He had been hooked up to a ventilator, a cardiac monitor, a central venous catheter, and an intravenous IV. He had looked like death. She had stood in shadow, shedding silent tears, not wanting to be detected. She'd watched in agony as Juelle leaned in to him and whispered in his ear, words Nora strained to hear but couldn't. She had waited for Sebastian to respond, a movement, anything, but there was none. She had waited, hoping Juelle would leave so she could sit by his side, let him know she was there for him, but a loud commotion in the hallway ensued, and she quickly hid behind one of the adjoining curtained cubicles as Sebastian's mother stormed into the room, shouting at Juelle. Thankfully Nora had been able to duck behind several empty, curtained cubicles in the ICU wing and escaped undetected.

She knew now Juelle hadn't been responsible for Sebastian's death. Still, her heart bunched at the angst and sadness she'd gone through. She shook her sad thoughts from her head, reached for her coffee, and gulped down several swallows, and then wiped the tears from her cheeks.

Oh, my God! Was Gavin lying in a hospital bed, dying? The man she realized she'd been starting to care about? The man she'd fallen in love with and wanted to spend a lifetime of happiness with, only to have it taken away? Gavin was nothing like Sebastian. She trusted Gavin. He was an honorable, honest man. He had feelings for her. He said he wanted to get to know her, when others in the community had given up on her. And at this moment he was probably out in the storm where something terrible might happen to him. Would anyone feel the need to call her?

She pulled her cell phone from her purse to dial Gavin's number when the office phone rang. Startled, she dropped her cell in her lap, then quickly picked up the ringing phone on her desk and prayed. *Dear Lord, let Gavin and his crew be safe!*

"Nora? Eric, here. Gavin asked me to call to let you know he's not going to be able to make dinner tonight."

"Is he all right? What happened?"

"He's fine. As we all are. A snafu out on the water this afternoon."

"Is anyone hurt? What happened, Eric?"

"Don't have time to fill you in. Things escalated today, and we had to call in the Coast Guard."

"Eric. Is anyone hurt? How is Gavin? Where is he?" She wanted to scream but controlled her emotions, hoping Eric would get to the point and tell her what had happened.

"Nora. Calm down. Gavin is okay. He'll fill you in later. I have to go."

"Eric. Where. Is. Gavin?"

Silence on the other end of the line. The urge to scream grew stronger. At least she'd gotten a phone call. But Eric hadn't really told her anything and had disconnected the call. The urge to jump in her car and rush to Gavin's side was overwhelming. But where would she rush to? Damn! Was she about to lose at love again due to a storm out on the Atlantic?

She snatched a tissue from the end of her desk and mopped up tears she hadn't realized she'd been shedding. A sob escaped. So much for status quo. She'd stepped over the line and trusted in love again, and it might be too late.

Before she talked herself out of it, she reached for the phone again, pulled it across the desk, and punched in Bethany's number. Beth's husband, Ed, was a cop. Cops knew everything when there was a disaster. Ed would know what was going on, where Gavin was, and if he was okay. And Ed would tell Bethany.

"Bethany, Nora here," she hiccuped. "I'm calling to find out what's going on with Gavin. He went out on the boat this afternoon to do more research, and something happened. Eric called, but he didn't give me any particulars. What's going on?"

"I was about to call you."

That was a surprise. As was Bethany's caring tone of voice. And the fact Gavin's sister thought to call her indicated Gavin might have talked to his family about their relationship, as he'd intimated.

She was holding on by a thin thread, her fingers tight around the receiver.

"Do you know anything?"

"First, Gavin is fine. There was a brief encounter

with another boat while Gavin was diving. With the storm and the boat kicking up waves, Gavin had a hard time surfacing and getting back on board. He has minor injuries, nothing serious. Al radioed for the Coast Guard, who then called in backup, and I guess all hell broke loose. Ed said everyone's back on shore. After a brief chase, the authorities apprehended the culprits. Gavin, Eric, and Al are being detained in order to give evidence. That's all I know."

"Thanks, Beth. I appreciate you letting me know. I've been worried, knowing he was out on his boat in this storm."

"Glad I could set your mind at ease. I know we didn't get off to a very good start, Nora, but if Gavin is serious about a relationship with you, I don't want to interfere. Family is important to him, to us."

Wow! Coming from Bethany, that was a major concession. Although, knowing how straightforward the entire family was, she wasn't totally surprised.

"I appreciate your honesty."

"While I'm being honest, you should know Gavin was devastated when his wife Celina died. He blamed himself for not being there when she needed him. He hasn't felt worthy of being able to care for someone else since. Lord knows I've tried to change his mind. But it hasn't worked. So for him to want a relationship with you must mean he's serious and willing to commit. Don't break his heart."

Again, wow!

"Thanks for sharing. Just so you know, I don't intend to be the one to break his heart."

"Good to know. I'm sure he'll be in touch as soon as he can."

Nora hung up and wiped her eyes with the back of her hand. She snatched another tissue and blew her nose. She had to get out of the office. Do something, other than sit around waiting to hear from Gavin. And heaven only knew how long that was going to take.

Deciding to finish packing the last of the items from the cottage and take them to her new home, Nora shut the office for the afternoon. There was an hour left, and things had been slow.

Unfortunately, Chuck was outside when she arrived at the cottage. There was no way she was going to escape a confrontation with him this time. Instead of waiting for him to approach, she took a deep breath, and deciding to stand her ground, hands on hips, headed his way.

"Listen, Chuck. I've had it with your innuendoes. If you don't cease and desist harassing me, I'm going to call the cops. Something I should have done a long time ago."

Chuck came to a screeching halt in the middle of the yard, his hand outstretched, held up in a stop sign as if he were afraid she would accost him. "Never meant any harm, there, Nora. You know I was just flirting with you."

"It was more than flirting, and you know it."

"Well, I thought you'd be a bit willing to share what you'd been sharing with Sebastian. Sorry if I read the situation wrong."

"I've never given you any reason, at any time, to give you the idea I was, or ever would be, interested in you, and you know it. Now. Back. Off!"

"Now, Nora…"

"The final check for the rent is in the mail. I'll

leave the key on the kitchen counter when I leave."

She turned, strode into the house, and slammed the door behind her. For good measure, she locked the door just in case Chuck decided to follow her. She waited half a second, then peered through the window to make sure he hadn't followed her. She quickly began to round up last-minute items, before taking one more quick check around the house to make sure nothing was left behind.

Thankfully Chuck was nowhere in sight when she returned to her car. Not wasting time, she loaded the last two banker boxes into the trunk, and without a backward glance, backed the car out of the drive and drove to her new home. Relief washed over her like a cleansing shower. Despite her worries, she couldn't help but smile as she left her past behind, something she should have done long ago.

Beside herself with worry about Gavin and having dealt with the confrontation with Chuck, she wanted nothing more than to have someone to talk to, someone to hold her, tell her everything was going to be okay. She missed her grandmother's loving arms. Arms she needed right now.

Half an hour later, she pulled into her own driveway, shut the motor off, and simply sat staring at her new home. Her home. A feeling of warmth, comfort, and independence filled her with possibilities she hadn't felt in forever. So much had happened since she'd met Gavin Redmond and started working for him. Who would have thought she would be accepted by the community, the McClintocks, and Gavin's family? And find someone who was caring, upstanding, pulled no punches, and was willing to work on an honest relationship with her. And love. She'd found love.

Nora entered her new home, tears streaming down her cheeks as she shut the door behind her. The peaceful silence surrounded her. She'd unload the boxes later. Instead, she strolled through the rooms, each one reminding her of Gavin. The living room where they'd kissed and almost made out in front of the sprawling fireplace. The bedroom where she'd envisioned them actually making love. Thinking of him being here in her home made her feel closer to him. Still, she couldn't wait to wrap her arms around him and feel his warmth seep into her.

Make sure he was okay.

He had to be okay!

Nora carted the rest of the boxes in and then put the tea kettle on to boil. A hot cup of cocoa was called for while she waited to hear from Gavin, even if it took all night. She settled next to the window overlooking the bay as the nighttime descended and the lights began to sparkle in the distance. The serenity mocked her chaotic thoughts. Was Gavin really okay? Where was he? What about the men who were responsible for the McClintock situation? Where they all rounded up? Was Gavin completely out of danger?

She leaned back on the settee and closed her eyes. And then it hit her. No one knew she had moved into her new home. Would he even think to come looking for her here? She should text him and let him know she had moved. Or would that seem too forward after her demanding they keep their relationship status quo? She could always call Bethany to find out what was happening. Still, she hung back until she couldn't stand it any longer. She decided to call Jackie when a loud knocking on her front door drew her out of her chair. She raced across the room, hoping against hope it was Gavin. She threw the door open and gasped.

Gavin filled the doorway, an angry bruise the size of a fist on his left temple as if someone had coldcocked him. His left wrist was padded and wrapped in an Ace bandage. He hesitated a millisecond before he stepped over the threshold and enfolded her in his arms. He kicked the door shut behind them as they melded into each other. His lips covered hers. The kiss consumed her, igniting a fire within her entire being. She wasn't ready for him to release her when he leaned back and shook his head. Confused as to his thoughts, she let him lead her in a daze-like state to the new sofa next to the fireplace.

"Are you all right?" Nora wiped at the tears streaming down her cheeks again, looking up at him as he tucked her in his arms. She ran her hand gently along his temple, brushing the hair aside. "Your head? Do you have a concussion? What happened? Eric didn't tell me a thing. Have you seen a doctor?"

"Slow down, slow down, sweetheart. I'm fine. A few bumps and bruises from being knocked against the boat when I was trying to get back on board, but nothing major. I've been checked out, and I'll live. I've lived through worse in the military."

"Oh, my God, Gavin, you have no idea the thoughts that went through my mind," she sobbed and laid her head on his chest. "I thought for sure something terrible had happened, and I'd lost you before I had a chance to tell you I love you."

He didn't give her a chance to say more. He lifted her chin, looked into her teary eyes, and kissed her. His good hand caressed her cheek before sliding through her hair, down her neck, and around her shoulders. He tugged her still closer and lowered his lips to hers. His kiss deepened, said more than words could say. But she longed to hear those three words. She pulled back, ran her hands through her hair, brushing it back from her heated face. Her body was on fire from his kiss, from his touch.

Gavin let out a deep satisfying breath, drew her back into the sofa, and in his arms. She snuggled into him.

"We need to talk," he stated.

Her heart beat double time, hoping he wasn't going to break it. She closed her eyes as he hesitated before he finally continued.

"But first, I want to tell you…I love you, too. I've been mesmerized by you from the beginning. I was so ecstatic to learn Bethany didn't send you my way. I couldn't help hiring you on the spot."

Nora sat up, brushed her smiling lips against his. "Oh, my God, Gavin, I was so afraid you didn't really love me, too. I was so taken in by you as well. But I've come to love your kindness, your generosity, and your love of giving back to the community. I think I fell in love with you almost immediately, too."

"I never thought I could love again," Gavin confessed. "Never wanted to. I felt as if I let my wife down. I wasn't there for her, and getting this business back on track didn't leave time for a relationship. But seeing you every day, knowing what you went through and how you held yourself up in the face of adversity, I knew I could love again. You are such a survivor. Your work ethics speak a lot for your integrity, as does your friendship with Jackie and Brad and their boys."

"It's true I've been ashamed of my behavior, Gavin, and I've hidden from life. But I also learned I couldn't have been in love with Sebastian like I should have been if it was true love. I would have been more hurt by his duplicity and unfaithfulness rather than the fact I was more hurt over how he died and how it made me look. I regret the time I wasted and the fact that I had been taken in by him."

"It's all behind us. Like we've said, lessons learned."

"You're such an honest, upstanding man. I know you wouldn't hurt me on purpose."

"I'll be there for you, I promise."

He kissed her again, and again. She melted into his embrace, oblivious of the time, the absence of light as the sun set for the evening, and they lost themselves in each other's arms.

So much for status quo.

****

Nora woke in the early hours, wondering when they had climbed the stairs and ended up in her new bed. She stretched, sated, and snuggled into Gavin's warm body and sighed.

He shifted, wrapped his arm around her, and whispered in her ear, "I'm afraid we've already passed status quo and hit the point of no return. And I can't say I'm sorry."

She turned and smiled up at him. "You do know I can no longer work for you."

"Why?"

"There is no way I'm going to be labeled as 'sleeping with the boss.'"

"Not a problem. I'll hire someone else. You can establish your own business. In fact, if you want, you can open shop next door to my office. I hear the owner is willing to rent."

"I happen to know you are the owner, and I don't want to depend on you for my livelihood."

"You did hear me say 'rent,' correct?"

"I can't afford to rent. I plan to work from home."

"But you'll continue to work for me until I can hire a replacement for you?"

"Does this mean I'll have to call in all those applicants to set up interviews for you?"

"Nope. I'm not interested in any of them. In fact, I have a friend that might be interested."

"Oh?"

"Don't even think it. Gwendolyn is not on the list, not even close. No, a friend of mine who is rotating out of the military is looking for work. I think he'll do a great job. That is if you really feel you can't work with me."

"I really want to make it on my own, prove I have what it takes. But I like the idea of you hiring a man to fill my spot."

"No one could ever fill your spot. Your spot is right here next to me. Always."

A word about the author…

Carol Henry is a #1 Best Selling author who lives with her husband in the beautiful New York State Finger Lakes area, where they are surrounded by family and friends.

Carol took an early retirement from Cornell University to write and travel the world. As a world traveler, Carol writes about her visits to exotic locations for major cruise lines' deluxe in-cabin books, and takes pleasure in sharing her adventures with her "characters" and readers in her romantic suspense adventure novel "Connection" series—Destination Romance—Exotic, Romantic Adventures—where the heroine discovers more than the "wild and wonderful" world around her—she finds her inner courage and a once-in-a-lifetime love. Carol also delights in writing contemporary and holiday romance novels.

~*~

Find Carol online at:

http://www.carolhenry.org

www.ingramcontent.com/pod-product-compliance
Lightning Source LLC
Chambersburg PA
CBHW072149170626
46813CB00004BA/1735